"Jonathan, let me in this minute. I mean you no harm."

The pounding started again.

"You'll like some of the games I'll teach you," the man called. "Let me in."

Jonathan stood there, saying nothing. Then abruptly the pounding stopped.

Jonathan found that more frightening than the noise. That meant the man was probably going to get tools to force the door open, or to get someone to help him, someone who wouldn't believe Jonathan no matter what he said.

He looked around frantically. Curtains lined the windows, but heavy as they were, they couldn't hide him.

There was a sound at the door. Jonathan whirled around. Whoever was on the other side was doing something to the doorknob. . . .

*Published by Fawcett Books

BUMP
IN
THE
NIGHT

Isabelle Holland

FAWCETT CREST • NEW YORK

To Wolff Computer
Where it all started

1

THE CHILD DISAPPEARED ON OCTO-
ber 14.

Martha woke up late, called her son, and then, when he
didn't answer, slowly and groggily got herself out of bed.

"Jon, where are you? Why don't you answer me?"

She paused, sure that she would hear his rather alto voice
if she just waited. But there was no sound except the drip
from the bathtub. The washer was old and she had meant to
have the plumber fix it, but somehow the days passed and
she forgot to call him.

"Jon!" She waited, slowly walking to the door.

"Jonathan, goddammit! Answer me!"

Suddenly the silence seemed to have a threatening quality.
Martha stood on the duplex landing orienting herself. It was
Saturday, she told herself; therefore her son, Jonathan, age
eight, should have been in his room. It was only—She glanced
at her watch and then stood looking at it unbelievingly. It
was ten-thirty. It should be only seven-thirty. What had happened to those three hours? She had waked at five with a

blinding hangover and taken both an Alka-Seltzer and a . . . a sleeping pill—

Oh my God! she thought. Then panic seized her. Stumbling down the rest of the steps, she glanced into the living room, the kitchen and the small study. Jonathan was nowhere.

Of course, she could have missed him upstairs, if he had decided to have a nap. An eight-year-old? Deciding to take a nap in the middle of a Saturday?

I must think, she told herself, continuing to stand there. Her head felt thick, as though her thoughts were trying to operate in some kind of congealed substance. "Coffee," she said aloud. Quickly she went into the kitchen, put on some water to boil, then came back to the living room.

Suddenly it occurred to her that Jon might be in the street, playing, something he was strictly forbidden to do unless he had asked permission and she was where she could keep an eye on him from the window.

"He had no right," she said aloud. And then grew self-justifying. "No right at all. He knows he's not allowed to play outside unless I've told him he can."

The phone rang, and at the same time the kettle started to scream. She let the kettle go on and plunged for the telephone, falling over Jonathan's cat, Susan.

"Get out of my way," she yelled, kicking out.

The cat gave a cry and rushed behind the sofa.

Martha snatched up the receiver. "Is that you, Jon? I want you to know—"

"Mrs. Tierney, please, this is Sarah Jennings."

"I'm sorry," Martha said, and made an effort to lower her voice. "I—I—" A sense of instant humiliation filled her. "I was back in the kitchen with the radio playing—"

"Mrs. Tierney, where is Jonathan? He's supposed to be in school. He should have arrived more than two hours ago."

"But it's Saturday." That reality seemed immensely important.

"It's Tuesday, Mrs. Tierney. And Jonathan should be in school. He should have been here at eight-thirty."

"But I thought—" Martha found herself staring straight at the wall calendar in the kitchen. Then she glanced at her watch, whose dial had a tiny square indicating the day. The little figure was twelve. The calendar straight ahead showed the twelfth to be Tuesday. Why on earth had she thought it was Saturday? Had the weekend disappeared in an alcoholic blackout? Couldn't she remember anything about it? Further humiliation washed over her, followed by fear. The fear rapidly became anger. She went instantly on the offensive.

"You mean to tell me that you—or at least his classroom teacher—have known for nearly two hours that Jonathan wasn't in school and you've only just got around to telling me?"

"She's a new teacher, Mrs. Tierney, and when Jonathan didn't answer to his name, one of the other kids said he thought Jonathan was visiting his father. I'm sorry."

"When I think of the fees I've paid to your school—" Martha could hear her voice, going on about their carelessness, the iniquitous amount of money the school charged per term, and her own anxiety provoked by their lack of efficiency and organization.

And then the ground was pulled from under her.

"Mrs. Tierney, we tried to call half an hour ago, but the phone didn't answer. We let it ring ten times."

Where had she put the phone in the bedroom? she wondered, and with a sick feeling remembered the times when she had got up, put a cushion over the telephone or put it in the closet or even in a drawer to keep it from waking her. Or perhaps it was just that the pill was still working powerfully.

"I forgot, I had to go to the doctor," she said haughtily.

"The main things is," the headmistress of the little private school said, "where is he?"

Martha was silent as she fought with nausea and with guilt, both overpowering. "Of course it's the main thing," she said. A terrible need to cry filled her, and she knew in one part of her mind that all of this was just a device for not letting the fact that Jonathan had disappeared get through to her. Because if it did . . . And then the full horror of what the headmistress was saying, of what she knew in her gut, hit.

Jonathan, her beautiful eight-year-old son, was missing, here in a city filled with criminals, sexual perverts. . . .

"Oh my God!" she said, and started to sob. "What's happened to him? Where's my little boy?"

"Are you alone?" The calm voice at the other end of the phone had its effect.

"Yes."

"Do you have a neighbor you can call. Or I can call for you?"

Beulah, the woman who lived in the apartment downstairs, worked during the day. So did both members of the couple upstairs. Several doors down there was Katie. Katie would be home.

"Yes. There's Katie Leonard. I'll call her."

There was a slight pause at the other end. Then, "All right. Call her. If she's not there, or . . . or not well, let me know. I'll send over one of the teachers. Now I'm going to see how much I can find out, and to question that child who thought Jonathan was with his father."

As she hung up, Sarah Jennings repressed a strong inclination to say, "And get dressed, have some coffee, and above all, don't have a drink." She didn't for one minute believe that Martha Tierney had been up long enough to be dressed and out. There'd been too many times when someone from the school had called only to get the same slurry, sleep-thickened voice, uttering similar unlikely excuses. But she was a woman who liked to choose her own time and place for a major battle, and the morning when Jonathan Tierney was missing was not it.

And besides all that, Mrs. Patrick Tierney was a fee-paying

parent. At a time when costs were going up, such were not to be insulted lightly.

St. Andrew's School, located on Remsen Street in Brooklyn Heights, was vaguely church-affiliated, small and coeducational. It had a good reputation and took its students up through the ninth grade. After that almost all the boys went to boarding school and the girls either did likewise or passed into one of the elite private high schools scattered over the Heights and the Upper East Side of Manhattan. Occasionally a particularly bright student with parents who were either financially limited or staunchly liberal or both sat for the tests to enter one of the competitive public high schools, such as the Bronx High School of Science, or Music and Art, or Hunter or Stuyvesant.

Sarah Jennings was always especially pleased when one of her stars went to one of those prestigious places, although she rarely recommended it. It took not only brains and scholarship to survive there, it also, in her opinion, required stability and toughness of spirit. The competition was—or had been before the recent, politically motivated relaxation of standards—fierce. And the bright city kids were not always noted for their civility or delicacy of feeling.

Jonathan Tierney would not be one of those she would expose to the city schools. He was a sturdy little boy, but she considered he had more than enough to cope with with his divorced and frequently absent father and alcoholic mother. He was also a child of great beauty, and the thought of that made Sarah's heart miss a beat. The list of children who had disappeared or been abducted was never far from her mind.

The main school building had been constructed in the earlier part of the century especially for St. Andrew's. But as the student body had grown, the need for more room had forced the school to take over brownstones on either side and renovate them for class use. Preschool, kindergarten, and the first two grades were housed in the brownstone to the north of the school. The third and fourth grades were in the brownstone to the south, and the remaining grades in the main building in the middle. The school stood flush with the street, which meant that the athletic field was three blocks off in a small private park.

Walking briskly now along the main downstairs hall, Sarah pushed open the connecting door to the brownstone containing the smallest children and went looking for Jonathan's homeroom teacher.

The third grade was on the second floor in the biggest and sunniest classroom. Sarah opened the door and went in. Fifteen eight-year-olds turned and looked at her and said, as they were drilled to, "Good morning, Miss Jennings."

Sarah knew that Hilary Babson, the new third-grade teacher now standing in front of the blackboard, encouraged such English-school-inspired manners. She wasn't quite sure how she herself felt about them. Part of her thought they were a phony import that sat ill on American children and that good manners involved more than these rather show-piece displays. On the other hand, she was astonished at how much pleasure the sound of the children's voices in their choral good-morning gave her.

"Good morning, children. Miss Babson, may I speak to you for a moment?"

"Miss Babson," she said, when the young woman emerged from the classroom, closing the door behind her, "I'd like to know again just how soon you realized Jonathan Tierney was absent. I know," she went on hastily, not wanting the relatively unknown quantity in front of her to take umbrage and become uncooperative, "that you informed me as soon as you knew yourself, but Mrs. Tierney is not an . . . an easy woman, and I don't want to give her any more reason for complaint than I have to."

"I'm sorry, Miss Jennings," Miss Babson said, a defensive note in her voice. "I would certainly have told you sooner, if I had not been assured by Stephen Morgan that Jonathan would most likely be with his father. In this day of almost universal divorce—"

Sarah had not known Miss Babson long, but she had

known her long enough to have a fair idea of her prejudices and preoccupations, since the younger woman was not hesitant at the lunch table or in the common room to voice them. So she interrupted now.

"I know how you feel about the breakdown of the family and the frequent separations. However, the main thing here is that the child be found."

"But why shouldn't Stephen be right? Why shouldn't I have believed him when he said Jonathan was with his father?"

"I understand why you assumed Stephen to be telling the truth. The trouble is, Stephen's parents are good friends of Jonathan's father, and rarely have a kind word to say about his mother. As far as they're concerned, custody of Jonathan should have been given to his father in the first place."

"Considering that she's a notorious drunk—"

"We're not discussing moral issues right now. Please call Stephen out."

"If you're going to punish him—"

Miss Jennings suddenly lost some of her patience. Opening the classroom door, she interrupted a low ripple of chatter and went in. "Stephen, would you please come out here for a moment."

"Told you it'd be about Jon," a girl said.

"And you, Marguerite," Miss Jennings said. Marguerite Stanley was bossy and pushy, but she was also bright and a good observer.

"Now," the headmistress said when both children came out, "why did you, Stephen, say you thought Jonathan was with his father?"

Stephen sighed and looked down at his feet. "I just thought . . ." he said. His voice drifted off.

"You mean you had no actual reason for saying so?"

"No."

"You hadn't heard anybody—like your parents—say anything? I know they're supposed to be good friends of Jonathan's father."

Stephen went on staring at his feet. Overwhelmed with the harm he could have done to the cause of getting Jonathan back to his father, he added, "He's a really super guy, and Jon'd a lot rather be with him than with his mother."

Miss Babson spoke with some indignation. "So because you wanted to believe something that we now know is not true . . ." She glanced at her superior. "It isn't true, is it?"

"No. No one has seen or heard of Mr. Tierney in some while."

"Yeah," Stephen said. "But he could be here couldn't he? And it'd be so much neater for Jon—"

"Wishful thinking is not reality, Stephen, and your saying what you did may have delayed our efforts to find him by an hour or two." It was also true that Mrs. Tierney wouldn't answer her phone for an hour, but Miss Jennings decided not to mention that.

"You mean he's really lost?"

"I mean that he's not at home, he's not here and no one knows where he is. Do you? I mean, do you really have any knowledge—not just fantasy—where he might be?"

"No." The little boy sounded desolate. "I don't. For real."

"All right, Stephen." The headmistress turned to Marguerite, a rather square child with a round face, bright green eyes and two stiff pigtails. "What about you, Marguerite? Do you have any idea at all where Jonathan might be?"

There was a pause. "No," she said.

Miss Jennings was fairly sure that Marguerite was not telling the entire truth, but when Miss Babson said, "Marguerite, I don't think—" the headmistress broke in.

"Forgive me, Miss Babson." She turned back to the stocky child. "I have a feeling you might have an idea of where Jonathan is. It's important, for his sake, that we know where to look."

Marguerite sighed. "Sometimes he goes to . . . to an animal shelter."

"An animal shelter?" Miss Babson's voice rose with astonishment. "Why should he go there? Does his father—"

"Why, Marguerite?" Miss Jennings said.

"Well . . ." Marguerite hesitated. She looked at Miss Jennings and then at Miss Babson.

Miss Jennings opened her mouth to say, "Please help us." But she didn't get the first word out.

"Well really, Marguerite," Miss Babson said, "I can't believe that that is where Jonathan would be when he is supposed to be in school."

Miss Jennings watched Marguerite's face close down.

"Marguerite?" she said gently. But she knew it was no use. To herself she cursed the clumsy teacher whose one approach seemed to be coercion.

"I dunno," Marguerite said.

"I think—" Miss Babson said.

"Miss Babson, I mustn't keep you here in the hall when neither of us knows what the children could be getting into."

It was not a statement laden with tact. But Miss Jennings was angry with the teacher and didn't mind showing it.

"Very well, Miss Jennings." And she swept past Stephen and Marguerite to open the classroom door.

"Stephen, is this something Jonathan talked to you about?"

"No. I think that's crazy. Why'd he go to the animal shelter?"

"Perhaps Marguerite can help us."

But Marguerite had been warned off any further cooperation. "I dunno," she said, and shrugged.

"Does either of you have any other idea?" she asked them. They shook their heads.

It was wisdom to recognize defeat, and Miss Jennings was a wise woman. "All right. Go on back, both of you." She was about to turn away when she suddenly thought of something. "Wait," she said. And then, when they had turned back, "Which animal shelter?" When there was no answer she said, "Marguerite?"

But Marguerite shook her head. "I dunno," she repeated.

"Please help us, Marguerite. Because it would be helping Jonathan."

Marguerite shook her head. "Dunno," she said.

"I don't know," Miss Jennings, frustrated, corrected.

Miss Jennings went back to her office and rang for her secretary.

"Joanna," she said, when that young woman appeared, "how many animal shelters are there in the Heights?"

Joanna Weldon was an attractive young black woman who was working her way through college, taking most of her classes at night. She could, Miss Jennings had told her often, have obtained a loan for daytime attendance, which would have cut short her time in obtaining a degree. But Joanna had an admirable and stubborn desire to graduate without a debt to be paid off. "And I'm not that much in a hurry," she said. "I'm not even sure yet what I want to do. And I like working here."

So Miss Jennings, feeling that she had paid enough tribute to her conscience, accepted Joanna's statement and rejoiced that she had someone as bright and well organized to keep her office functioning.

"I'm not sure there are any shelters in the Heights," Joanna said now. "I think the nearest city shelter is in the Flatbush area, or maybe Park Slope."

"I gather there are other than city shelters."

"There are various private types who pick up strays and try and find homes for them." Joanna looked with sympathy at her boss's worried face. "Why are you interested? You're not thinking of giving up Alcibiades, are you?"

Alcibiades was Miss Jennings's cat, a large black neutered male.

"Of course not." She glanced at Joanna. "Are you aware that Jonathan Tierney is missing?"

"Yes. I think that's pretty much around the school now."

"When asked where Jonathan might be, Marguerite suggested an animal shelter."

"But she didn't say which one?"

"I'm afraid she got interrupted before I was able to ask her that."

"Marguerite's aunt, the one she lives with while her parents are abroad, sometimes takes in strays."

"Not, I hope, like that crazy Beauchamps woman. Doesn't she live in the same area?"

"Yes, she does. But Meg Stanley's not as bad as that. Nobody knows how many cats Miss Beauchamps has; she won't let anyone in to see. Meg isn't nutty. Just a little soft in the head about animals."

"Well, she'd obviously be a good person to talk to. Let's get her on the phone. Or does she work?"

Joanna was about to answer when Miss Jennings glanced towards the window. "Oh Lord!"

"What's the matter?"

"Mrs. Tierney is here."

Martha had somehow got herself dressed. All the while she was putting on her clothes and at the same time trying to control the shaking of her hands, she told herself that this once she would not take an early morning drink. She would not take it because Jonathan was missing—temporarily, she assured herself—and because she was sure that when she got to the school that nosy, self-righteous headmistress would smell it on her.

But then, just before she left the house, she knew that she wouldn't be able to get through the coming hours without a little something to hold her together. The shaking of her hands was so bad she could see her purse jumping around. So she had two shots of vodka, because vodka wasn't supposed to have any odor.

As she waited after swallowing the second shot, anticipating the sense of calm and control that would come, the voice of her divorced husband, Patrick, sounded in her mind, as it often did. "Why the hell do you think I'd want to leave

my son with a woman who can't stay away from the bottle?''
His voice was so clear she turned her head, expecting him to
be there. But he wasn't.

Oh God! she said to herself and shivered, even with the
reassuring warmth of the vodka. Custody of Jonathan had
remained with her because of Patrick's constant traveling. A
former journalist, he still spent months abroad each year on
research for his books. But one day, book or no book, he
might decide to stay home, especially if he became convinced that she hadn't managed to put some kind of hold on
her drinking as she had sworn to him—and to the judge in
the custody case—she was going to do. She shivered again,
reminding herself that Patrick was due back in two weeks.
As soon as Jonathan was home safe she'd really come to grips
with her drinking.

The thought of AA drifted across her mind. Who had first
brought it up? Maybe it was that interfering brother of Sarah
Jennings, David Jennings, whom she had met somewhere.
A member himself, he had suggested she might like to go
with him to a meeting. She had refused flatly. "I'm not an
alcoholic," she had told him. She repeated it aloud to herself
now. "I'm not an alcoholic!" Her drinking, she reminded
herself, was the immediate result of Patrick's scurrilous behavior. Even before they separated he had made no secret of
the women he wined, dined and bedded. She'd have it under
control by the time he got back. Her hands had stopped shaking, so she wrote a quick note to Jonathan, telling him that
Katie Leonard three doors down had the apartment keys,
then spent a few minutes frantically looking for her own set
that she normally kept in her handbag. This time she found
them in her sewing box. Then she called Katie.

The phone rang eight times, but Martha let it ring, since
she knew that Katie, like herself, had a hard time getting up
in the morning, and for the same reason. A rush of affection
for Katie filled her. It was good to have a friend who wasn't
always criticizing her and suggesting she had trouble with
alcohol.

"I'm not an alcoholic," she repeated aloud. And at that moment Katie picked up the receiver.

"Hello," she said foggily.

"Wake up, Katie," Martha said. Then she added, "Jon's missing." And started to cry.

"There now," Katie said. "I'm sure you've just forgotten where he is. Now think!"

"He's not at school, and that moralistic beast Sarah Jennings called to tell me. I'm on my way there. I've left a note on the door telling Jon, if he comes home while I'm at the school, to come over to you. Is that all right?"

"You know it is, Mart."

"So don't go back to sleep on me, will you?" She added, "Have a shot of vodka."

"I might do just that," Katie said, sounding brighter.

Martha left the note on the door and walked over to the school as fast as she could. She had put on high heels, because she always felt more formidable in heels, but they kept her from moving too rapidly. Her ankles turned easily, and on the uneven pavements of the Heights she had to be careful.

"But why would he go to an animal shelter?" she protested when she was in the headmistress's office.

"I don't really know, Mrs. Tierney. I was hoping you might cast some light on that. But Marguerite Stanley is a friend of his and she seemed to think it was a possibility."

Miss Jennings was fully expecting a stubborn argument, so she was surprised and pleased when Martha said, "Which one? There must be dozens." Obviously, the quick mind that had once made Martha Tierney one of the city's best journalists was still—occasionally—functioning.

"We don't know. Joanna, my secretary, says that Marguerite's aunt runs a sort of unofficial shelter herself. Maybe we ought to start there."

Martha sat down and rubbed her forehead. "If Jon were at the Stanleys', then Megan Stanley would have called either you or me." Sarah was about to reply when Martha said,

"We might as well call her anyway." And before Sarah could move, picked up the phone in Sarah's office. "What's the number?" she asked.

Silently, Sarah turned the Rolodex to Mrs. Stanley's number and watched Martha punch out the number.

"Yes," Mrs. Stanley said cheerfully, "Jon was here."

"When?" Martha shot back, her voice hostile.

"Around twenty to eight. He said he came to look at the new kittens."

"And then he left?"

"Yes."

Sarah, who had gone to Joanna's extension to listen to the conversation and add her two cents if she thought it was necessary, said, "I have one more question. Did he say what he was going to do when he left?"

"He said he was meeting his friend before school."

"Which friend?" Sarah and Martha said together.

"How should I know? He simply said it was a nice man he'd met, a friend of his father's, who was going to buy him breakfast. I figured that, as usual, he didn't get any."

"What time was that?"

"Around five to eight. Isn't he there yet?"

"No."

"Well, maybe he's enjoying his breakfast for a change."

"And you didn't think to call and check, or at least tell me?" Martha shouted.

"What good would that do? You probably wouldn't be out of bed, and if you were you probably wouldn't be sober." And she hung up.

Sarah noticed that by now Martha was a ghastly color, a greenish white. Below her eyes were purplish brown shadows, made all the more obvious by puffiness. Many years ago, Sarah reflected, when they were both at Smith, Martha as a student, she as an assistant in the English department, Martha had been a beautiful young woman, tall, leggy, with auburn hair and an enviably slim body. She was still tall and leggy, though the bulging abdomen above her thighs made her look fat and cumbersome. Even her hair seemed to have faded to a dull brown, periodically streaked with brassy blond stripes. How are the mighty fallen, Sarah thought, and reflected wryly on the long reach of her biblical upbringing. "Do you have any idea, Mrs. Tierney, who this friend of Jonathan's father could be? This, quote, nice man that he was supposedly going to meet?"

Numbly, Martha shook her head.

"Not a cousin or brother-in-law or uncle or anybody who could be reasonably considered to have connections to you and Jonathan?"

"No."

"Is there the slightest chance it could have been Jonathan's father?"

The familiar fear shivered through Martha. There was so much she had to do before he was due back. She moistened her lips. "He's in Europe. My lawyer told me that and said he'd return in two weeks." If not— But she didn't want to think about that, and besides, nothing mattered until Jonathan came home.

"In six hours, let alone two weeks, he could be back in New York. Have you heard anything of him since you talked to the lawyer?"

Martha shook her head again. "No."

"So it could be his father."

"Why would Jon call him a nice man?"

Sarah answered slowly, "Maybe he did it deliberately to keep anyone from knowing he was going to meet his father." She added, "I take it you have complete custody of Jonathan."

Martha gave a sob and buried her face in her hands.

Sarah stared at her with a mixture of compassion and contempt. "Does that mean yes or no?"

"It means," Martha said, raising her head and speaking with a forlorn dignity, "that we share custody. But because

Patrick travels the agreement was that Jonathan would live with me—unless I got drunk again.''

"And then he would live with his father.''

Martha nodded. "Yes. If he stopped traveling and came back here permanently.''

"Then we have to assume it was his father he was meeting.''

There was a pause. For Martha, the thought that Jonathan might be with his father—the man who had so contemptuously rejected her—was unbearable. "I still don't think so.''

"Why?''

Martha was too fuddled and frantic to give a rational answer. She just shook her head.

"That's a big help. I'm going to call the police.''

2

PATRICK TIERNEY SAT IN THE DOUGH-
nut shop on Court Street drinking his fourth cup of coffee. It
was, he decided, probably the worst coffee he had ever tasted,
including the bilge handed out in second-class English hotels, with which, as a writer doing research that took him to
some of the smaller towns of Great Britain, he had intimate
acquaintance. He stared down at the watery liquid. He preferred his coffee black, but with this brew he had added milk
on the theory that any change could only improve it. His
theory was wrong. If this were one of those English hotels
he would now order tea. English tea was as magnificent as
some English coffee was dismal, but American tea vied with
the worst of English coffee. He pushed the cup away and
looked at his watch for the umpteenth time.

Jonathan had said he would meet him here at eight. The
words of Patrick's lawyer, spoken almost every time they
talked and most recently yesterday afternoon, filled Patrick's
mind. "Whatever you do, don't, I beg you, *don't*, try to see

Jonathan without asking his mother first and setting up the date with her permission.''

"His mother's a drunk," Patrick had said savagely. "Trying to have a sensible conversation with her—one that she'll remember the next day—is like catching air in a—a sieve.''

"I don't care, Pat. The name of the game is your getting custody—that is, if that's what you still want and you're going to stay put for a while. You can't have custody if you're out of the country three quarters of the time. It's not fair to the boy. But after the last report from the detective agency, your chances are excellent. Martha's drinking has escalated in the past six months, and, according to her neighbors and the school, Jonathan goes around alone as though he were twelve, not eight. She's not fit to have him, and we can make a strong case for your having custody. That is,'' the lawyer went on, underlining the words, "if you behave yourself. Having titanic fights with Martha is not the way. You remember what happened last time you were home!''

Patrick winced. A year before, he had called on Martha to suggest a) she cut down on her drinking, b) she try a rehab and c) while she was there he'd take Jonathan abroad with him.

He had barely mentioned his first suggestion when she exploded in fury. He raged back. Almost everyone in the entire house heard, and Jonathan, after screaming, "Stop! Stop!'' had fled from the apartment.

When the battle was over and Jonathan had finally been located at Marguerite's, Pat had appealed to his lawyer.

"Public arguments aren't good for anyone's cause,'' the latter pointed out.

"It wasn't public,'' Pat said stiffly.

"It might as well have been, and making Jonathan run away did nothing for your side.''

"She was drunk.''

"You don't even have that excuse.''

After that, Patrick had (reluctantly) promised to be good, which included his not trying to get in touch with Jonathan without first talking to Martha. "In the long run you do yourself more good that way," the lawyer explained patiently. "Technically, you have the right. Realistically, it's better to get Martha's cooperation when you want to call Jonathan and talk to him or take him out. You'll get further that way."

Since then, Patrick had been in England and France. But the previous day, fresh from Europe, too beaten down by jet lag (he told himself) to embark on careful negotiations with Martha and yearning to see his son, he had succumbed to temptation and telephoned Jonathan in the hope that it would be he who picked up the phone.

And that time he had.

"Son, don't say anything."

"Hi!" Jonathan said with such warmth and enthusiasm that Patrick felt tears spring to his eyes.

"Hi, Jon," he said, and was embarrassed to find his voice shaking.

"Are you okay—er, okay?" Jonathan had almost let slip the fatal word, "Dad," but caught himself just in time.

"I'm fine. Don't you worry about it. Listen, can you meet me sometime? Anywhere. Just say the place."

Jonathan was no stranger to guile. Living with his mother had taken care of that. But at that moment he heard her coming slowly down the stairs. He could often tell to within an ounce how much liquor she had had by the sound of her voice or her steps, and he was quite sure now she had had enough to be drunk but not enough to pass out.

"Meet you at the doughnut place on Court Street at eight tomorrow," he said quickly, and hung up.

"Who were you talking to on the phone?" Martha said.

"Just Joey."

"Oh." She seemed to search her mind. "What did you say you were going to do at eight?"

"Go to gym class together."

"Oh. All right."

Patrick now glanced at his watch. It was eight-fifteen. He had taken the trouble to make sure that this was the only doughnut place on Court, though he remembered there were several on Montague. And, of course, there were any number of things that could have delayed a small boy who was trying to get away from a difficult mother and perhaps avoid other nosy adults or children. To distract himself, Patrick eyed the obvious renovations in the doughnut shop, to which his attention had been drawn by the smell of paint.

At nine Patrick was still sitting at the doughnut shop table, holding his newspaper clenched in his hand as though it were a weapon.

At nine-thirty he tried to call Martha. There was no answer.

He had several times considered phoning the school. But he had learned from bitter experience that calling the school without talking first to Martha produced wild scenes when Martha found out about it, which she always did. He gave as good as he got in those scenes, but with his lawyer's advice ringing in his ears he preferred not to precipitate another—at least not for the moment. And it was always possible that, unknown to Jonathan, Martha had made an appointment for him this morning with his doctor or dentist, and, given the secrecy with which Patrick himself had wrapped this morning's date, Jonathan would not be likely to tell his mother.

Then another thought intruded, frightening him. Could Jonathan have been in an accident on the way to the doughnut shop?

Patrick got up abruptly, started to leave the shop, then went back to speak to the counterman.

"If a little boy, eight years old, reddish hair, comes in, tell him I'll be back. I'm his father."

The man looked up from his paper. "Sure."

Patrick walked the length of Court Street and back and then went to Montague. Could Jonathan have meant one of the doughnut places there? Half an hour later he had gone into every doughnut place. No one had seen a boy answering to Jonathan's description.

At ten Patrick headed for the nearest phone to call the school, scene or no scene.

Jonathan Tierney had gone to the doughnut shop on Atlantic Avenue.

After he had hung up the phone, he was so excited over the prospect of seeing his father and also so frightened that his mother might have heard his part of the conversation and guessed whom he might be talking to, that when the morning came he left a little early and decided to stop by and see the Stanley kittens on his way to Court Street. There he found Mrs. Stanley distracted with worry about Simpson, her big ginger male, who had taken to hiding under the bed for absolutely no good reason. She was also fairly sure he was not eating much.

"I wonder if I should take Simpson to the vet right away," she said.

"Why don't you?" Jonathan asked, sitting cross-legged among the kittens. Gently he removed one of the kittens from his head, where it was playing with his hair, and got up to leave.

"Because he loathes the carrier and I sometimes think that no matter what's wrong with him, he's more traumatized by being put in it than by whatever ails him." She glanced up and took in the fact that Jonathan, uncharacteristically, was departing almost as soon as he had arrived. "Off so soon?"

"Yes."

"To school?"

"Actually . . . I'm going to the doughnut place on Court Street."

"At this hour? Why didn't you say you were hungry? There're some muffins in the kitchen. Anyway, the place on Court Street is closed for renovations."

"Are you sure?"

"Of course I'm sure. I passed by there a couple of days ago. Were you going to meet somebody?"

Jonathan was overcome with an urge to mention his father. With a huge act of will he pushed it back. "Yes."

"Anybody I know?" Her eyes were back on Simpson, who had opened his mouth and seemed to be panting. "There *is* something wrong with him. Oh God, the last time one of my cats did that it was Amanda, and she died the next day. I'll have to take him to the vet now. Help me, Jonathan. He likes you. Hold him and talk gently to him while I get out the carrier. Oh, he's going to hate this!"

For nothing else would Jonathan have delayed his departure, but a cat was an animal and therefore more important than any person, except his father, and he'd just have to run when he finally got out.

They eased the protesting Simpson into the carrier and Jonathan helped Mrs. Stanley lug the carrier to her car parked on the street. "I'd offer to give you a lift, Jon, but I think the sooner I get Simpson to the doctor the better. It's not Marguerite you're going to meet, is it? She didn't say anything."

"No, it's a nice man." The need to mention his father became overpowering. "A friend of my father's."

Mrs. Stanley was placing the carrier gently on the passenger seat, her murmured words to the cat drowned out by Simpson's loud protests.

As she started the car and turned away from the curb she knew that something about their conversation had bothered her, but she couldn't concern herself now with digging it out. Simpson was making ominous sounds that usually meant he was about to throw up. Fretting and worrying over Simpson, she forgot about what had disturbed her in Jonathan's comments until she found herself talking to Sarah Jennings.

Jonathan ran, zigzagging towards Atlantic Avenue in the hope that when he discovered the place on Court Street closed, his father, who hadn't lived in the Heights for three years, would have inquired as to where the nearest doughnut shop might be and then gone there. Of course he might just stand in front of the closed shop and wait. But it seemed much more likely to Jonathan that an important and highly intelligent man like his father would not do the obvious thing that any ordinary man would do. He'd figure out that Jonathan probably meant another place nearby and would find out where it was and go there.

Martha had often accused his father of fiendish subtlety— a quality she particularly disliked, especially when she had a hangover. And there were times, when she was displeased with Jonathan, that she suggested he had inherited that unlovable characteristic. Jonathan was extremely proud of it. He tried to be as subtle as he knew how.

Jonathan's only watch was on the fritz, so he had to guess how late he might be by checking clocks as he ran past drugstore and other windows. Unfortunately they didn't agree. According to one he'd be exactly on time. To another, he'd be ten minutes early, and to two others, a quarter of an hour late.

He slid into the doughnut shop on Atlantic Avenue and looked around. The clock there reassured him. He was only five minutes late, and given the fact that his father didn't know Brooklyn Heights well, he couldn't be expected to be on time. Jonathan sat down and started shredding a napkin that had been left there.

Time passed. Jonathan stared at the clock, which seemed not to have moved. This proved, he told himself, that he had not waited as long as he thought. A watched pot never boils.

"You waiting for somebody, son?"

Jonathan stared at the man standing beside his table. He was dressed like most of the men around the Heights, including the men teachers at the school, in tweed jacket and jeans. If he had had on a pinstriped suit, Jonathan would have been instantly on his guard. He did not consciously take on his mother's opinions and prejudices. But as far back as he could remember, his mother was given to talking with scorn about corporate Nazis in pinstripe suits.

"Yeah, my dad."

The man had a thin face that in some way reminded Jonathan of his father's, although his father had brown hair and this man's was black and his father had blue eyes and this man's were brown. Maybe, Jonathan thought, it was the nose, a prominent beak with an aquiline bend. Whatever it was, it gave Jonathan a slight feeling of reassurance.

"I think," the man said, "he was here looking for you. He hated to have to go, but said to tell you he'd be in touch."

"What time is it?" Jonathan cried. Disappointment flooded through him. He felt sick.

The man looked at his watch. "What time were you supposed to meet him?"

"At eight. But the clock there says it's only—" The obvious fact that the clock wasn't moving now struck Jonathan with stunning impact, along with his own stupidity in wanting it to be right. "Oh no, oh no!" he said, hitting the table.

"I'm afraid it's long past eight. I'm really sorry."

Jonathan sat there with his arms on the table, flattened with misery. He had been less than six when his parents split up. Since then he had seen his father only half a dozen times. The main reason, he knew, was that his father was so often out of the country. But even when he was there, Jonathan didn't see him as much as he would have liked to, and this he blamed on his mother who, while she couldn't prevent their getting together, would frequently be deliberately obstructive.

"Jonathan, that's the afternoon we're going to the pediatrician, don't you remember? You can't go out with your father then."

"Can't we change it? You already said I could spend the day with him."

"Well, I forgot. We're going to have to make different arrangements for you to go out with your father. It's almost impossible to see Dr. Penrose."

Eventually, he'd get to see his father. But eventually usually included a fight, and while his mother would not drink the day he was to see his father, she would the next and the next to make up for it.

After the divorce he was content to live with his mother. At that time her drinking had not damaged the early close-ness between them, those years when she read to him, played with him, and took him to the zoo and the aquarium. His father, brilliant, impatient, was somebody to adore, but not somebody to count on as being there when Jonathan needed him. He'd be likely to be off in Africa or Asia pursuing some story. Having his parents divorced, Jonathan told himself again and again, wouldn't be different.

But it had been. Not because his father's pattern was any less erratic, but because his mother's drinking had suddenly escalated. The woman who had read to him after school and at night became a sullen, silent creature, glass in hand, star-ing at the television set, erupting in anger whenever his father returned to New York and wanted to see his son.

Now, numb with disappointment at his father's failure to show up at the doughnut shop, he directed his anger towards his mother, because it was unthinkable that this disaster could be his father's fault. If there was any way his father could have waited for him, he would have. If he, himself, hadn't stopped to help Mrs. Stanley with Simpson, he would have been on time. . . . But Simpson was a cat, like Jonathan's own Susan. If her cat was ill, then she was right to do every-thing to help him, including delaying Jonathan. His mind veered back to the acceptable target. If his mother weren't such a—a rotten person . . . Aware that tears were trickling down his cheeks, he got up from the table and stalked out of the doughnut shop. Once outside, he furtively wiped his cheeks with his hands.

"What do you plan to do now?" asked his father's friend, who must have come out with him.

Jonathan shrugged. He could, of course, go to school. He'd be late by now, and there would be questions. And the headmistress, Miss Jennings, would call his mother. Jona-than rather liked Miss Jennings, but he knew that he couldn't stop her from getting in touch with Martha if that's what she thought she ought to do. And his mother would almost certainly berate him in the alcoholic rage that seemed to have been so frequent in the past six months.

"I think I'll go to the zoo," he said. As always, animals would comfort him. He had fought a long, hard battle to have Susan, and his mother had given in only when the pedigreed Siamese had arrived as a present with a full batch of papers. Martha still didn't like animals, but insisting that an expensive pedigreed animal be given to a shelter was more than she could do, particularly as the cat came from her own sister.

"I think the zoo is an excellent idea," the man said to Jonathan. "Where is it?"

"Prospect Park."

"Of course! I'd forgotten there was a zoo there. Would you mind if I go with you?"

Jonathan had a vague feeling that it was not a good idea to let this man get friendly. There had been lectures at school about the dangers for young children in talking to people they didn't know, let alone going somewhere with them. On the other hand, he had been chosen by his father to carry a message to Jonathan.

"Where did you know Dad?" he asked, instead of answering the question.

"From business."

"You mean you're with his publisher?"

"Yes." The man put his hands in his pockets and strode beside Jonathan, his long legs making the strides look easy.

Detective Sergeant Pete Mooney listened to Sarah's crisp voice on the other end of the telephone giving him the outline of Jonathan's possible disappearance.

"I say possible, Mr. Mooney, because of course Jonathan could come walking in at any moment, having decided to skip school this morning. But it's not like him. His mother is"—she glanced at Martha's face across the room—"distraught, and I wondered if you had any people who could help organize a search."

"You say he just failed to show up this morning at school?"

"Yes. But as I said before, it's not like him."

"What time did he leave home?"

"I'm not sure. But he was at a neighbor's before he was due to show up at school."

"Do you or his mother have any idea who he might have skipped off to meet? I mean, if the parents are divorced—By the way, are they?"

"Yes, they are, and I asked his mother that question. The answer is, she doesn't know. The last she heard from anyone about her husband was two weeks ago when she talked with her lawyer. At that time she learned her husband was in England."

"Well, he could have come back here the next day."

"That's what I told her."

"So this kid could have gone to meet his father."

"Yes."

Mooney doodled on a pad beside his phone. When missing children were involved, it had been his observation that in nineteen out of twenty cases a missing child could usually be found with the divorced or separated parent. That didn't mean that the anguish of the parent who had been left was any less. A missing child might very well be with the non-custodial parent, who meant nothing but good. But the parent left in the dark struggled against the savage mental picture of the twentieth time, when the child had been kidnapped or lured away by a stranger. Those were the heartbreak cases. Because he was a divorced parent whose only child lived with his former wife and in some respects seemed lost to him, he dreaded those more than anything else, and had to fight against an unwillingness, as each case came up, to acknowledge the possibility of the stranger involvement. It was so frequently hopeless and, in his opinion, worse than death, both for the parents and for the child.

He said now to Sarah, "The first thing is, don't panic and don't decide the worst right now. Give me a description of the kid and I'll get it on the radio right away. What's his name?"

"Jonathan Tierney."

"Age?"

"Eight."

"Height?"

"About four feet and three or four inches."

"Weight?"

"Seventy pounds."

"Coloring?"

"Red-blond hair, gray eyes."

Mooney wrote down the answers, a mental picture of the child Jonathan forming in his mind. Almost angrily he thrust it away. Just because it was a child he must not allow himself to sentimentalize the case. For one thing, it would impair his judgment.

"Why did he stop off at the neighbor's, and who is she?"

Sarah sighed. Along with her anxiety was a growing irritation at Martha Tierney and her uselessness. It was worse than pointless to turn on Martha and berate her for her poor care of her son—for not knowing what time he left the house and where he was going. Not only would it not find Jonathan, it would probably muddle what little common sense and powers of observation Martha had left.

"I think he wanted to see some kittens she had. Her name is Megan Stanley. She also lives on Sidney Place. Her niece, Marguerite, is in the same class as Jonathan."

"I'll have to talk to his mother. You say she's distraught. Is she there with you?"

"Yes. Do you want to talk to her?"

"Yes."

"All right." Sarah turned, holding out the receiver. "Martha? The policeman wants to talk to you." A conscientious woman, she reproved herself for harboring a tinge of malicious pleasure in the fact that for once, in talking to the policeman, Martha Tierney would have to cope with something herself. As Martha came forward she handed her the receiver. "You can sit here."

"Hello," Martha said.

"Mrs. Tierney, I'm sorry about your son. Do you know at about what time he left your house?"

From Martha's viewpoint it was the worst question he could have asked. If answered truthfully, it would reveal the hangover, the drinking the night before that had brought it on and the sleeping pill early in the morning. She hesitated. The simple truth, "I don't know because I was still asleep," formed in her mouth. But she couldn't bring herself to say the words. "I guess around seven-thirty. He wanted to see the kittens at the Stanleys' before school."

"But you don't know the exact time."

"No." She found her tongue adding, apparently of its own accord, "I was in the shower."

"All right. I'm coming by the school now and would appreciate your staying there."

Mooney put down the telephone and glanced up at his partner. "I'm going around to St. Andrew's School. One of their kids hasn't showed up."

"Lucky you. Divorced parents?"

"Yeah."

"He's probably halfway to somewhere else with the parent he isn't living with."

"Yeah. That's what I think." Or what I hope, he thought.

Lawrence Miller walked beside Jonathan fighting the internal battle that always seemed to be with him and that escalated the moment he became in any way involved with a male child. One side insisted, I mean him no harm. He wouldn't be sitting in a doughnut shop by himself at eight in the morning if he was decently looked after. Kids today are neglected. Parents don't care. If Michael had lived . . . The other side, the side that never seemed to express itself in words, was drinking in the beauty of the little boy, the red-gold hair, the sensitive features, the guarded look in the widely spaced gray eyes.

"Do you have any animals of your own?" he asked when Jonathan, who had been chattering on about the tigers in the zoo, had run down.

"Yes, Susan. She's a Siamese."

"Seal point or blue point?"

"She's a lilac point," Jonathan said proudly. "She was almost completely white as a kitten and her ears and nose were pink. For a while I called her Miss Pink."

"How old is she?"

"She's two. She has blue eyes that are slightly crossed and a loud voice. When Mother—" He stopped. He was about to say, "When Mother trips over her . . ." But a vestigial sense of loyalty stopped him.

Lawrence's senses quickened. He was sure that midsentence brake meant that the boy was probably going to give out with some candid and uncensored information about his mother. Lawrence had a profound conviction that old-fashioned, caring motherhood had gone out, if indeed it had ever existed. And that children, especially boy children, were neglected.

"When Mother what, son?" he asked gently.

"Well, sometimes Susan stands in front of her and Mother trips." Technically, this was true. But saying it that way angered Jonathan. Loyalty was loyalty, and what about his loyalty to Susan? "I mean, Susan doesn't mean to stand in front of her. Anyway, she has a loud voice."

"Siamese often do. They're famous for it."

"Do you have a Siamese?"

"No. As a matter of fact, where I live now, I'm not allowed to have a pet."

"That really stinks."

"I agree with you."

Lawrence had a sudden mental picture of the seedy single room he was now occupying. Once his home had been a house in a college town with a garden and a dog and, yes, two cats wandering around. But they weren't Siamese. One was calico, one was black. "I had two cats once," he said now. "But neither one was a Siamese."

"What were their names?"

He could hear Michael's voice: "Let's call the kittens Scylla and Charybdis." And Donna's amused voice: "Do we have to be so literary? Why not Blackie and Smudge?" It was true that Michael was precocious, and he'd just been telling his son about the legend—

"Maybe we ought to get a bus," Jonathan said, suddenly interrupting his memory. "The park's pretty far."

Lawrence was flung out of his dream into potential danger. Buses contained people who had nothing to do but sit and remember those around them.

"It's such a nice day, why don't we walk? It's not that far. And we'll be all the hungrier for a hot dog when we get there." He watched the boy's face closely. Michael had loved hot dogs. This boy's expression didn't change, didn't show pleasure. "Or an ice cream." This time there was a slight lifting of the boy's mouth. But he didn't say anything.

Lawrence didn't trust silences. They gave people—like this boy—too much time to think and remember warnings against talking to strangers. Casting around rather desperately for something casual yet personal to say, the teacher in him came up with, "By the way, there are several spellings of your name and I forgot to ask your father which one you used. Which is it?"

"I never heard of any except mine," Jonathan said.

"Really? As I said, I can think of three. He could feel the moisture breaking at his hairline. Why the hell did the kid have to be so seemingly poised, so plainly—from the way he spoke and acted—from an educated background? Why couldn't he have been an ordinary street kid from a working-class area? And if, Lawrence asked himself, he had wanted a kid from the working class, what was he doing in Brooklyn Heights, probably the richest neighborhood in all New York except the Upper East Side of Manhattan?

I didn't want—I wasn't looking for—a boy, one of his internal warring parties seemed to scream in his head. Liar! the other side mocked. You were looking for this boy, the boy in the pictures that seedy man, Ben Nicolaides, in that squalid hangout sold you, this beautiful kid with the troubled eyes that you've been stalking for days. . . . And then this morning he finally saw him come out of one of the houses and talk to a woman before she drove off. The boy looked, Lawrence told himself, as though he might need a friend. Also, in some way, he reminded Lawrence of Michael, though Michael was dark and taller. . . . He snapped to as he heard the boy spelling his name. "What was that?" he asked quickly.

"Like I said, J-O-N-A-T-H-A-N. What are the other spellings?"

Relief made him weak. "Oh, an *o* in the final syllable rather than an *a*," he said.

"What's the third?"

"An *o* in the middle instead of an *a*."

"I never heard of that."

"They're not really common ways of spelling it," he improvised rapidly.

Jonathan, the man thought, Jonathan. *I am distressed for thee, my brother Jonathan: very pleasant hast thou been unto me: thy love to me was wonderful, passing the love of women.*

The ancient words brought a sentimental ache. Watch it! he told himself. Soon, but not now.

"Do you happen to have a picture of Jonathan with you?" Sergeant Mooney asked Martha.

She pawed in her large handbag. "I never can find anything," she muttered, still heaving things from one side of the bag to another.

"Maybe a school picture?" Mooney said, turning to Sarah Jennings.

Before he even asked she had pulled the most recent yearbook from the shelf. "I'm not sure—No, we didn't get one of him. He had flu the week the children were getting their pictures made. I told him to bring one in, but he never did."

Martha was strongly tempted to say, "He never asked me about it." It was true, she had no recollection of his ever mentioning the matter, but she knew she couldn't be sure that her memory was reliable, so she decided to say nothing about the school picture. Instead, she finally and triumphantly pulled a wallet out of her bag and flipped it open. "Here it is. Taken only . . . well, only three years ago. I've been meaning to get another one."

Three years, Mooney thought, would bring the eight-year-old back to five years. What could you tell about an eight-year-old boy from a picture taken when he was five?

"Let me see," he said, reaching out for the wallet. There, in its plastic envelope, was the photograph of a small boy with straight red-gold hair falling over his forehead. The face underneath the hair was round and serious. "Do you think you have a more recent one at home?"

Did she? In her desk drawer there were boxes full of snapshots, unless those were the boxes she had put on the top shelf of her closet, or maybe they were among the boxes that she had persuaded her landlady to let her store in the basement.

"No," she said loudly, because it was easy and wouldn't ambush her with sudden demands on the part of other people who wanted to see pictures she might or might not have. "No. I sent all the photographs of him to my sister who wanted to see them." Then, because she felt that everyone in the room was silently accusing her of lying, she said, "That was last year."

"So neither of you has a recent picture of Jonathan," Mooney said. He tried not to sound judgmental, but it was, in his opinion, a hell of a note when neither of the two people most intimately connected with the missing boy had a photograph that could help him in his search.

"I'm afraid not," Sarah Jennings said.

"No," Martha said more baldly.

"I guess I'll have to ask his father," Mooney said. "Do you know where I can reach him?"

It was at that moment that the buzzer on Miss Jennings's telephone sounded. She went over and picked up the receiver. "Yes, Joanna? Oh, all right." She pressed down a button on the telephone and said, "I'm glad you called, Mr. Tierney. We were about to try to get in touch with you." She glanced towards Martha. "No, I'm afraid he's not here."

3

THE LOOK OF DISGUST ON PATRICK
Tierney's face when he walked into Sarah's office and saw
his former wife was like a slap in the face.

"Still on the bottle, I see," he said. "Couldn't you at least
lay off enough to get my son safely to school?"

"You have no right—" Martha started shrilly, when Mooney interrupted.

"Let's leave the accusations for the moment. We have to
locate a child."

"We wouldn't have to if he'd been halfway looked
after—"

"Mr. Tierney." Mooney addressed himself to Patrick because he felt there was a greater chance of progress there
than with the befuddled woman who was Jonathan's mother.
"Right now we don't have time to waste. Whoever's fault it
was, the important thing is to find out where your son is."
He paused, then added, underlining the words, "Everything
else has to be postponed—no matter how you feel. Okay?"

Patrick stared at him. "Of course," he said. "For now."

35

Mooney went on, "When were you last in touch with Jonathan? I take it you were supposed to meet him this morning." Out of the corner of his eye he saw Martha about to speak and turned towards her suddenly. She closed her mouth.

"I called Jonathan last night, around nine," Patrick said. "He told me to meet him at the doughnut shop on Court Street at eight this morning. I got there at about five minutes to eight and waited for him until nine-thirty. Then I thought he might have meant one of the doughnut shops on Montague Street and checked all of those. Nobody'd seen him. So then I called here."

"Do you have a recent photograph of your son with you?" It was a long shot, Mooney thought. If the boy's mother, who had custody of him, couldn't rustle up a recent picture, where would his father get one? Still, you never knew.

Patrick hesitated a second, his lawyer's words still sounding in his brain. But Jonathan was missing. Beside that, nothing mattered. "Yes. Here." He reached into his coat for his billfold and opened it. There, behind the plastic frame, was a snapshot. He pulled it out and handed it over. "It was taken six months ago."

Mooney looked at the photograph. It was a head shot and almost certainly enlarged. The five-year-old's round face was now thin, the cheekbones high, the eyes wary. An astonishingly good-looking boy, he thought, though not a happy one.

"You don't have custody of your son, do you, Mr. Tierney?"

"We share custody, but I travel a lot so he lives with my former wife." His voice hardened. "For the moment."

"But when you're home you can see him freely?"

"When obstacles aren't put in the way."

"What obstacles?" Martha snapped.

Patrick went red and then white. "You have one hell of a nerve asking that!"

"Shall we keep to trying to find your son, the son of both of you?" Mooney interrupted coldly. "Time is passing. If he has been . . . has fallen into the company of a—a stranger, the sooner we can figure out how to find him, the better." He paused, letting the pictures his words summoned up have their effect. "All right," he went on. "How did you get this picture, Mr. Tierney?"

"I bribed a kid who works in my agent's office to hang around the school and take it and send it to me."

Mooney stared down at the photograph. "Was this the only picture he took, or were there others?"

"There were others. This was the best."

"Do you think you could get hold of the others?"

"Sure. Why? I mean, will more be better?"

"I'm not sure I can tell you why. But I'd still like to see them." He turned to Martha Tierney. "When did your son leave the house this morning?"

"I told you. I was in the shower."

"Approximately?"

As Martha continued not to answer, Mooney was fairly sure of the reason. He had seen too many alcoholic women not to be able to identify one. There were the coarse pores on the skin, the body appearing bloated without being actually fat, the uncared-for look, the bloodshot eyes. . . . Despite everything he felt sorry for her.

Martha raised her head and looked at him with despair. "The truth is, I overslept. He . . . Jonathan left the house before—before I got up. I wasn't well during the night." The pathetic lie lay there, obvious to everyone. "Oh God!" she said and put her hands up to her face. "Oh my baby."

Mooney glanced back at Patrick Tierney. If looks could murder, Martha Tierney would be dead. And Mooney could understand that, too. He turned to Sarah. "You say that this Mrs. . . . ." He looked at his notebook. "Mrs. Megan Stanley said that he had arrived at her house to see some kittens. What time would that be?"

"She said about seven-thirty. And left about five minutes to eight. She also said . . ." Sarah hesitated briefly. "She said Jonathan said he was going to Court Street, where he was going to meet a friend. He described him as a, quote, nice man, close quote. He said he was a friend of his father's.''

''What?'' Patrick said.

Mooney turned. ''Did you tell him it was all right to say where he was going? Or did you tell him to keep it to himself?'' He knew that in these ugly custody cases parents were inclined to be secretive and paranoid.

Patrick's mouth clamped together for a moment. ''I told him to keep it to himself because I didn't know what trouble his mother might raise. Yes, I know, Martha, I'm not supposed to make any inflammatory statements about you, but if your attitude hadn't been a factor I wouldn't have had to tell him to keep his mouth shut.''

''So it's all my fault, as usual. You're the one who made dates with him when you knew he was supposed to be in school, who hired people to spy on him and photograph him—''

''Which I wouldn't have had to do if you had had the decency to send me copies of his most recent pictures.''

''Okay, you two,'' Mooney interjected. ''I wonder why Jonathan felt impelled to say anything about, quote, a nice man. That seems a pretty odd thing to me.''

''Maybe . . .'' Sarah started.

He turned. ''Maybe what?''

Sarah hesitated. ''Maybe he just felt impelled to mention his father and, knowing he shouldn't, said something less dangerous but still satisfying.''

''Why should he do that?''

''Children like to talk about something they're excited about. So they'll sometimes go at it sideways.''

They were all silent for a moment. Mooney put away his notes and faced the parents. ''I think you both ought to go on home in case your son tries to reach you.'' He turned to Patrick. ''Would he know where to get in touch with you?''

''Yes. I gave him the telephone number in the last letter I wrote.''

"Okay. Then I think you'd both better be at home. I'll talk to you later."

"I'd like to know what the kids here say," Patrick said.

"So would I," Martha joined in, in rare agreement.

"If there's anything, I'll tell you. But I'd rather see them alone." He turned to Sarah. "Could you send for them?"

Lawrence Miller walked slowly beside Jonathan as Jonathan stared into the cages they passed and commented on the animals.

"Those tigers look sad," he said, peering between the bars at a huge tigress spread out on the ground, head on her paws. "Do you think she hates to be in the cage?"

"She has some space outside, where the tigers roam around the field over there. Maybe she's here because she wants to be." Surreptitiously he glanced at his watch. It was now ten-thirty. Experience told him that with a boy of Jonathan's age missing, the police would already be informed. Descriptions of the boy would be broadcast to every police car. In the zoo they were better off than in the streets, at least for the time being. But that could change as the news of Jonathan's disappearance got out. He'd better hurry things up.

Once again doubt overwhelmed him like a subtle enemy. It's been so long, he told himself. Self-pity flooded through him. So much had been taken away. He meant the boy no harm.

"Look," he said. "I didn't tell you this before because I didn't want to get you too excited. But your father told me that if he had not joined us by now, we were to go to him, and I think we ought to find a cab and go."

"Why didn't you tell me before?" Jonathan cried.

"I told you, because I didn't want for you to be too excited and start insisting we go to him right away."

"I'm not a baby!" If there was anything that enraged Jonathan it was someone, usually his mother, treating him as though he were younger than he actually was. "I'd have understood. Where are we supposed to meet him?"

Lawrence had prepared himself for this question. "At a house where he and his agent are going to meet another writer and another agent. They're there to discuss a special writing project they're both engaged in." Silently he thanked the fates that Ben had been able to tell him about the father's profession.

Jonathan frowned. "Dad always said he'd never go in with another writer on a book. He says it almost never works. And anyway, how did he know we were going to be at the zoo?"

Sweat started to break out again on Lawrence's hairline. Why couldn't this boy have been stupid? "Because he was quite sure that the zoo would be the place you'd want to go. You always go there when you're disappointed and upset."

"Yeah, I guess." Jonathan then added proudly, "He knows me pretty well, doesn't he? Even though he doesn't see me a lot. He knows me a lot better than—" Again he stopped.

"Than your mother?"

"Yeah."

Lawrence felt an upsurge in self-justification. Here was obviously a mother who didn't care, and her neglected son who needed someone to love him. . . . "Let's head to the gates, okay? I'm sure we'll find a cab there."

But when they approached the gate there were no yellow cabs in sight, and as Lawrence looked around he saw what he had been too preoccupied to notice before: the area was poor and almost entirely black. No wonder there were no yellow cabs. Then a dark car with the word LIVERY stuck in the windshield approached. "Here," Lawrence said, "We'll take this."

"That's not a cab," Jonathan objected.

"Yes it is. It's just a different company. In with you!" He pushed Jonathan into the back of the car, went to the driver's window and said quickly and in a low voice, "102nd Street

sharp edge in his beloved's voice—something he managed to forget most of the time. He straightened. ''Because we said to meet here. Remember?''

''Only after you said you didn't like the Shamrock. What've you got against it?''

The Shamrock was not the kind of bar featured in Barry's fantasies. The latter summoned up comparisons with the King Cole Bar in the St. Regis, or the Oak Bar at the Plaza, cocktail lounges where his boss's secretary was constantly telling clients to meet her employer. ''Mr. Fremantle said to meet him in the Oak Bar at five-thirty,'' she frequently said over the phone to a privileged author or an important Hollywood contact. ''He usually sits in one of the corner booths. Just say you're meeting Mr. Fremantle and the headwaiter will take you there immediately.''

Barry had been to the Oak Bar himself now twice. The first time was when a hand-delivered letter Mr. Fremantle was waiting for arrived just after he left the office to meet a client for dinner. ''Take this to Mr. Fremantle in the Oak Bar, Barry,'' the secretary said. ''He wants to get it tonight. Do you know where it is?''

''Sure. Plaza Hotel.''

''Okay. Here it is. Get moving.''

Just going to the Plaza had set his heart beating. As he neared the sacred premises of the Oak Room he thought he'd suffocate. A headwaiter bore down on him with a chilling look, but when Barry said he was there to deliver a letter to Mr. Fremantle, the waiter's face thawed and he waved a hand towards the agent's table.

The literary agent, a well-mannered man, thanked him and then introduced him to Patrick Tierney. ''As I'm sure I don't have to tell you, Barry, Mr. Tierney is the author of *Focus*, one of the most successful books we've handled. And this is Barry Pinkus, who messengers for us while he's getting his degree.''

''Hi!'' Patrick said. ''Where are you studying?''

''Baruch.''

"Good for you."

Focus, an intricate and riveting story of international intrigue, had not won the Pulitzer Prize, but it had been made into a successful movie. For Barry, meeting Patrick Tierney was almost the equivalent of meeting the Pope for a devout Catholic.

"You worked on the screenplay, didn't you Mr. Tierney?"

Patrick smiled, and his intense, rather bony face, relaxed. "For my sins. Writing the novel was a picnic by comparison."

"Don't let him fool you, Barry," Fremantle said. "He turned out to be a born screen writer. I'm going to scribble a note on the back of this envelope and I'd like you to take it back to the office. I think Janice will still be there."

Speeding out of the Oak Room he had not heard Fremantle say to Patrick, "The kid has enough ambition for a killer whale, but what he's really good at is photography. He ought to go into that instead of dreaming of Hollywood."

But by the next day Barry knew such an exchange had taken place, because while he was chewing his sandwich in his cubbyhole near the reception office, Patrick Tierney had strolled in and offered a proposition: an assignment to take some photographs of Tierney's son, Jonathan. "Look," Patrick had said, taking out a map of Brooklyn Heights. "Here is where Jonathan lives, and here is where he goes to school. The name of the school is St. Andrew's, and it's on Remsen Street. You could snap the shot there either in the morning or at the end of the school day. It'd be easier, of course, to take him coming out of his house, but . . . well, I'm afraid his mother might see you, and there'd be hell to pay."

So Barry had taken his camera to Remsen Street early one morning, had fixed it with a telescopic lens, and had snapped away while Jonathan loitered talking to various friends. Barry, hiding across the street in a doorway, had not been noticed. Taking the camera back, he had developed the pictures himself and carried them into Fremantle & Coe the next day. Patrick had been delighted. With his pencil he had drawn frames around the parts he had wanted enlarged, and when that was done, had paid Barry handsomely.

On the strength of that money, Barry had taken Cheryl to the Oak Bar, cautioning her to dress properly.

"What're you talking about? I always dress right."

"Well, no punk stuff," Barry had said. "That place is full of class."

For all her defiance, Cheryl had been impressed. Finally she asked the crucial question: "Where'd you get the money for a place like this?"

Barry had never boasted about his photography because that was not where his ambition lay. But he knew he took good pictures and told her about his assignment from Patrick.

"You sure it was his kid?" Cheryl asked. She was older than Barry and her professional life had lain along paths he had hardly dreamed of.

"Sure I'm sure. Why else'd he want the pics?"

"He might be one of those men. Men who like boys."

"I told you, this is his son. He took out an old photo of the kid and showed it to me. It was all he had, but it was about three or four years old."

Cheryl shrugged. "So you could recognize him?"

"Yeah. A good-looking kid. Maybe a little, well, sensitive. But you couldn't miss him even in a crowd of other kids."

"Got any copies of the pics?"

"No, I gave him all the positives. Why?"

Cheryl lied. "I'm thinking of taking drawing lessons again. I used to do it in school. A picture of a nice-looking kid'd be something to help me. Better than a real kid, because they're never still."

"Okay. I still have the negatives. I'll bring you some glossies next time we meet."

Cheryl had looked at them. Barry had been right. The kid was good-looking, almost beautiful. She knew who'd pay good money for those photos. "Gee thanks, Barry. These'll help a lot."

For all his smattering of street smarts, Barry had a broad streak of naïveté. He liked to call himself a New Yorker, which was accurate in that he came from New York State. But he was not from the city. Barry had grown up in a small town outside Rochester. What Cheryl saw immediately she could do with the photographs was something that would not have occurred to him in a thousand years.

Now he said, "I thought we said we'd meet in front of the administration building. It's near Joey's, where they have great beer and sandwiches." In fact, he was embarrassed to admit to his dislike of the Shamrock. But he found the people there sleazy and a little frightening, and he didn't care for the way some of the men looked at him. Not for anything, though, would he have said this to Cheryl. She had an uncomfortable way, sometimes, of looking at him and pronouncing judgment on some of his statements. "That's not cool, Barry." One of the things he liked about Cheryl was her air of having been around.

As they munched their sandwiches at Joey's, Cheryl asked casually, "Hey, you got any more pictures of kids? I mean, the photos you gave me really help. I was thinking I oughta have more. Like, they're different and it'd give me more experience."

"No. I once thought about going into photography, but agenting is the place to be now."

Cheryl chose her words carefully. "Y'know, I think you could make some money with pictures of kids. I mean, like, agents are always looking for them for commercials and so on. I know a couple of people from work who do photos for them."

"Yeah? Well sure, if you know any kids who want to break into television or Broadway, I'd take their pictures."

This wasn't exactly what Cheryl's business partner had in mind. What he actually said was, "Tell your pals I'll buy pictures of kids this good-looking anytime. There're never enough for the market.''

The business partner worked in a filthy-looking walk-up in one of the side streets between Broadway and Seventh Avenue. Ostensibly it was a place that developed ordinary snapshots at a discount, and tourists, attracted by the SAME DAY, 40% OFF sign, dropped film off there constantly. But behind the cut-rate front and up one flight was a full floor, divided into cubicles and a couple of studios. Clients came there for something else. Painted on the windows facing the street were the words BALLET SCHOOL, and music—usually familiar ballet music, but sometimes rock—sounded constantly. This explained the children, both boys and girls, but mostly boys, going in and out of the doorway.

For the umpteenth time Cheryl wished Barry weren't such a square. He was a sweet guy and better in bed than most of the men she'd slept with. But she stuck to him because there was something about him that gave her confidence in his ultimate success. If, in the meantime, somebody with more success up front happened on the scene, she'd leave Barry in a minute. Barry was a good-looking boy, and sometimes she wondered why he stuck with her. She knew she wasn't pretty. What she didn't fully realize was that in her almost anorexic thinness she had an entirely false air of fragility, and it appealed to a romantic streak in Barry that still existed under his layers of hastily acquired sophistication.

Cheryl now tried to figure some way to get Barry to find handsome boys, photograph them and bring the pictures back to her.

''You know, you could just take your camera along in the street, snap good-looking kids, get their names and addresses, and if the people at the commercial agencies want them, well, then it's a nice surprise for them.''

Naïve as he was, this suggestion rang some faint alarm in Barry's mind. ''Just take pictures of kids whether or not they want it?''

Cheryl pushed her empty dish back and got up from the

table. Barry might be a pushover, but she had to be careful. One push too many and she might be in trouble. "It's up to you. Just thought you could use the money. Commercial agencies are always looking for cute children for their ads. And some of them would kill to get on television. I have to get back now. Thanks for the lunch." And she marched out of the restaurant, confident that Barry would be so upset if she seemed displeased that he wouldn't think of anything else. She was right.

"Hey!" Barry said, throwing some money down on the table and going after her. "Maybe you're right. Maybe it is a good idea!"

He was behind her so he didn't see the look of satisfaction that crossed her face.

Neither did he see the man who rose up after they did. The man had been stalking Cheryl all morning. Now, also leaving money on the table, he followed them out.

4

MARTHA PACED BACK AND FORTH IN her living room. It was a few minutes past one. She had been at home an hour, following the suggestion of that sadistic policeman, Mooney, that she should be there in case Jonathan came home, or in case he or someone else called.

It was the "someone else" part that she found sadistic.

Actually, Mooney had said, "Maybe you ought to go on home. Jonathan would go there if he were just coming back from some outing or adventure or spree, or some—someone might call about him." He made an effort not to sound punitive or threatening. Martha heard the slowing of his words as a deliberate effort to inflict pain.

"Bloody sadist," she said aloud, and then, again, "Bloody sadist."

The words served for a moment to buoy her up. Then her spirit caved in. If she had just not overslept. If she had just not drunk herself into a zombie state last night, sitting in front of the tube. What was it she had been watching? She couldn't remember. She passed out around eleven and then woke up around four with the dry heaves. She retched long past the time when there was anything left to bring up. That was when she had taken an Alka-Seltzer and a pill and had slept until . . . until Jonathan was gone.

"Oh God!" she whispered, and, as though pulled, her eyes went across the room to the cabinet where she kept the liquor and where two bottles, one of bourbon and one of vodka, were sitting on a tray on top of the cabinet.

The desire—no, far more than that—the craving for a drink blotted out everything else, even, for a moment, the pain about Jonathan. The drink would unquestionably make her feel better, think better, function better. . . . She was almost across the room when something within her, something new and implacable, said in her mind, as though somebody else had uttered the words, You Cannot Drink Now.

It was not a decision she was making. It was a decision that had been made.

She turned away and started pacing again. Then the phone caught her eye. She could call the school to see if any news had come. . . . She could call— Who else was there for her to call?"

"Please bring him home!" The words came out of her like a cry. And then, "Please let him be all right!"

To whom was she praying? She had gone from being a devout believer to an angry agnostic. "All religions are the same and they're all crap!" That had been a line used more than once in some of her barroom arguments.

Always when she was slightly drunk any conversation turned to cosmic issues. Why I Believe in God. The God I Believe In. Finally, The Belief in God Is the Longest-Running Myth in the History of the World. It was a long title, but it had style, and many of the evenings in front of the television set were spent polishing some of its arguments. Not on paper, just in her head. It was a talk she would deliver one day when she was finally recognized as one of the better writers and thinkers of modern journalism, one of the victims of the sexism that continued to rage in the world of newspapers and news magazines. . . .

"Please let him be all right. Please let him just be playing hooky."

She found herself once again within feet of the liquor bottles. One drink would make her think more clearly, feel better, be better able to help in this awful crisis, help her perhaps remember something that might yield a clue—

Her hand was reaching out when the phone rang. Obviously God had stepped down and prevented her from picking up that drink. She ran over and lifted the receiver. "Hello?" Her voice came out high and panicky.

"Martha?"

"Pat. Have you heard anything?"

"No. That's why I'm calling. You'd be more likely to hear than I. Have you heard from Jonathan or from anybody about him?"

She shook her head and then realized that he couldn't see. "No."

"It's no use asking you about anything he might have said this morning. What about last night? Do you remember anything?"

"Last night? What kind of thing?"

"Use your head, Martha. Anything at all he might have said if he planned to go somewhere today."

What did they do yesterday evening? The last part was pretty much a muddle. But in the earlier part . . . She remembered pan-frying some chicken legs for a casserole and then chopping tomatoes and celery and thawing some peas. . . . A picture of her kitchen appeared in her mind. Where was Jonathan? She saw herself, a big knife in one hand, holding the tomato in the other, and off to one side, a glass with dark gold liquid. And lying full-length on the other end of the table, Susan hoping for a handout.

"Jonathan and I had dinner here." She wanted to add, "I cooked it." But it would sound ridiculous.

"And he was there all evening?"

The sharp impatience in Patrick's voice, a sound that was once all too familiar but which she hadn't heard for a while, provoked anger and self-pity. "Yes, he was here all evening."

Was he? She remembered his helping her put the dishes in the dishwasher. She remembered his going back to his room to work. What did they talk about at dinner? It was a blank.

"I can't think of anything he said that had any bearing on where he is now," she said. There was a silence. Then Martha asked timidly, "Have you heard anything? What—what does the policeman say? Mooney, what does he say?"

"Nothing. You and I left at about the same time because he wanted to talk to the children alone. Remember? I came home, and I haven't heard from him since and neither has Miss Jennings. I called and asked her. Look, here is the phone number you can reach me at: 555-4766."

"That isn't the number to your apartment."

"No. My apartment is sublet and will remain so for the next month. Right now I'm subletting one myself. If you hear anything at all, call that number. If I'm not there, there's a tape. If there's any problem you can always call Roger Fremantle."

He was about to hang up when Martha said, "Pat—"

"Well?"

"Do you think Jon's going to be all right? I mean, a kid often goes off this way, doesn't he? You were a boy once. Boys do this more than girls, don't they?"

Even as she talked, Martha knew that she was pleading subserviently, begging for reassurance, and hated herself for it. "I mean—"

"You mean you want some reassurance that everything's going to be all right. I'd like that, too, Martha. But I'd like it even better if I could have the reassurance that by some magic you'd become a responsible mother, somebody with whom I'd feel safe leaving my son, since the idiot courts

seem to feel that a mother—any mother at all—is preferable
to a father. If I hear anything I'll let you know.''

The moment he hung up Patrick was sorry for his next to
last comment. For one thing, it wasn't entirely true. As he
well knew, his own absences had a lot to do with Martha's
having custody. And there was no point in weighing in on
his former wife at this point. Furthermore, reproaches would
probably wipe out what little memory and ability to think
she had left. But his anger, that had lately seemed bottom-
less, bubbled up when he least expected it.

He was in a small flat sublet to him by a friend who was
spending the season in L.A., and for a moment, to his intense surprise, Patrick wished he were in the Brooklyn
Heights apartment. He and Martha had lived there for eight
years—three before Jonathan was born and five afterwards.
And he would have sworn that its bitter memories for him
had erased the good ones. But there *had* been good ones,
before Martha had crossed some invisible line to alcoholic
drinking, before he started staying out the night with somebody else. For a moment he saw Martha as she had been four
years previously—bright, articulate, funny, sexy—a woman
who could still excite him. There had been some good years,
before and especially after Jonathan was born, years when
the three of them did things together—had picnics, went to
the zoo and the aquarium, strolled on the promenade opposite the soaring jumble of downtown Manhattan. Both he and
Martha were making good money, and the duplex on Sidney
Place, although expensive, was well within their combined
income. Now he had to maintain it for Martha and their son.
Fortunately, he had made money on his most recent book so
it wasn't much of a strain.

He got up. Waiting was godawful. He stared at the photograph of Jonathan in a leather traveling frame that was now
beside his bed. It was another of the ones taken by that kid,
Barry something, employed as a gofer by Roger Fremantle.

Pat stared at the phone, then jerked up his arm to look at

the time. Nearly one. The kid was probably on his lunch break.

Patrick was downstairs trying to hail a cab before he knew what he was doing.

Actually, Detective Mooney was ahead of him. Armed with Barry's name and the address of Patrick's agent, he had gotten into his car and driven into Manhattan. Fremantle & Coe were on Greenwich Avenue in Greenwich Village, an avenue that lay athwart the strict rectangular grid that marked the midsection of Manhattan, slanting from Sixth Avenue and Eighth Street to Eighth Avenue at Fourteenth Street.

The Fremantle office was on the fourth floor of what had once been two brownstones that had been joined together. In the front was a reception office and off it a room not much larger than a closet, where the messenger sat and which also served as a mailroom.

When buzzing from below, Mooney had, on impulse, simply given his name. No need, he thought, to announce that he came from the police. He had no reason to think there was anything amiss with the gofer who took the pictures of Jonathan, but who knew how the boy might react? And who knew also how many back doors there were to such an old place?

Fremantle's secretary, who also doubled as the office receptionist, pressed the bell to let him in without demanding credentials—not, Mooney thought, the safest practice in a city like New York. On the other hand, a literary agent could very well have clients, authors, and assorted others coming in at all hours and couldn't always demand they wait at the door to be properly identified.

When he got in, he asked the receptionist, "Do you have a messenger named Barry Pinkus here?"

"Sure. He's out now with some packages, but he ought to be back soon." She eyed the policeman. "Who wants him?"

Mooney took out his identification and showed it to her.

"Wow! What's Barry been up to?"

Mooney smiled a little. "Nothing, as far as I know."

"Well . . . you can sit there if you want to. He shouldn't be too long."

Mooney sat down in the chair in the waiting area and tried to be patient. The boy, Jonathan, had been missing only a few hours. Mooney reminded himself that the chances that there was anything wrong were a hundred to one. Dozens of children in New York wandered off every day, giving their parents and their schools the fright of their lives. And then they came back wondering what the fuss was about, or were found playing hooky.

But there were the others, the ones who did not come back. Mooney knew their names, and they filed past in his mind.

Roger Fremantle, on his way from the men's room outside the office, came through the reception area and saw a tired-looking man in his forties in a poorly fitting suit sitting there patiently, looking at a notebook in his hands.

"May I help you?" Fremantle asked.

Mooney stood up. "I'm waiting for your messenger, Barry, Barry Pinkus, to come back." He paused. "I'm Detective Pete Mooney." And he took out his identification again.

Fremantle glanced at it. "Why do you want Barry?" He was surprised. Barry had seemed a squeaky-clean kid, surprisingly so in the late eighties in the city of New York.

Mooney was taking in the handsome, rather nattily dressed literary agent. About forty-five. WASP. Such classifications were inevitable and meant nothing to Mooney except as a filing system.

"I believe he took some photographs of Patrick Tierney's son, Jonathan, for Mr. Tierney. Did you know anything about it?"

"No. But that doesn't mean anything." He paused. "I do remember mentioning to Pat that Barry took excellent photographs."

"Have you talked to Mr. Tierney in the last couple of hours?"

"No. Why?"

At that inopportune moment Barry burst through the front door. Seeing his boss and another man talking in the small area, he skidded to a stop.

"Why?" Fremantle persisted.

"Just a moment, sir." Mooney turned to Barry. "You're Barry Pinkus?"

"Yes."

"I'm Detective Mooney." Mooney pulled out his identification again. "Did you take photographs of Jonathan Tierney during the past week or so?"

Oh God, Barry thought. Some nosy, interfering neighbor of the school had complained. Was it against the law? "Yes. I did. Mr. Tierney asked me to. What's wrong with that?"

"Nothing, as far as I know."

"Detective Mooney, why are you asking these questions?" Fremantle asked sharply.

"Because Jonathan's father and mother and the school are concerned. Jonathan hasn't been seen since about five to eight this morning."

"My God!" Fremantle said. "You mean he never turned up at school?"

"No. A neighbor saw him when he came to look at some kittens in her apartment around seven-thirty. Then he left at five to eight, saying he was supposed to meet a friend at a doughnut shop on Court Street. It seems the so-called friend was his father, who had made a date to meet him at the doughnut place at eight. Mr. Tierney was there, but Jonathan never showed up."

"Oh Christ!" Fremantle turned to the receptionist. "Get Patrick on the phone for me, Sheila."

Mooney turned back to Barry. The boy had gone completely white. Mooney cursed the fate that had brought Fremantle out to the reception area when he did. Mooney would have led up to the subject in a more circuitous way.

"No reason to be frightened," he said. "You didn't do

anything wrong in taking the photographs. Did you, by the way, show them to anybody?''

"No," Barry said. In the few seconds between the cop's first question as to whether he had taken the photographs and this last one Barry had come to a difficult but necessary decision. He had to protect Cheryl. He knew there'd been vague trouble in Cheryl's young life. She'd never been too specific about her reasons for mistrusting police, but one thing was clear: she was in no way to blame.

"Just because you stick up for your boss," she said once to Barry, "they look on you like a . . . a criminal."

"Police are as corrupt as anyone else in New York," Barry had said, quoting Pinkus senior, who found paying the mob for protection for his small cleaning establishment was in no important way different from paying the local police, which he also had done. Anyway, Cheryl must be protected against unfair pressure.

"No," Barry said firmly. "I didn't show them to anybody. And I developed them myself."

"I thought Dad's agent lived in Greenwich," Jonathan said. There was an edgy note to his voice.

"His house is there," Lawrence said quickly. "This is just an apartment where he entertains clients—he keeps it for business."

Lawrence could feel Jonathan's rising anxiety. The boy was becoming suspicious. Once again Lawrence asked himself bitterly why he couldn't have been interested in a slower, less sophisticated child. He had to get Jonathan to the apartment soon. Fortunately, there were only a few more blocks to go until they reached 102nd Street and Broadway. (He had not dared to give the driver the exact address. Cab drivers were required by law to record such addresses, and he didn't want it noted down anywhere.) Once they reached the corner, they'd be almost at the apartment, the address and keys of which had been given him by Ben Nicolaides, the man who sold him the pictures of Jonathan. Lawrence didn't like

Ben, and he didn't want to take Jonathan to the apartment Ben was supplying. He wanted Jonathan for himself for as long as he wanted him. He would treat him like a son, a much loved son. . . .

But there were practical problems. Lawrence no longer had a place where he could take a boy like Jonathan, a place where he and the boy would be safe from prying neighbors. Even in a city like New York, neighbors could be a nuisance. But Ben, who owned the studios off Broadway that Lawrence patronized from time to time, had offered this apartment. "It's an old place," he'd said. "We use it for filming some of our deluxe stuff. The walls are thick. You and the kid could be there for a while and nobody'd be the wiser. Then I'd know where to find him when I needed to start some work."

"All right." Lawrence tried not to think about how much he disliked this particular man, his dirty fingernails, his leering eyes and heavy mouth. He wore a diamond ring on his little finger and his clothes emitted a musky perfume. Lawrence's feeling for this boy had nothing in common with the sleazy traffic the man specialized in, Lawrence assured himself again and again.

"You mean Dad's agent has an apartment up here?" Jonathan asked as the taxi passed through a particularly rundown block. Astonishment and doubt filled his voice. He was a New York City boy, born and bred. He knew about neighborhoods, whether in Brooklyn or Manhattan. And there was nothing in the neighborhood of Amsterdam Avenue and Ninety-ninth Street, through which they were now passing, that indicated it might be a place where the elegant Mr. Fremantle would live. Almost everyone in sight was either black or Hispanic and all were plainly poor. Jonathan was free from racial and ethnic prejudice. But, like most New Yorkers, he was snobbish about neighborhoods.

"We're just going through it," Lawrence said. Again he could feel the sweat on his face and under his arms. Then, as so often happened in the city, the cab traversed a few blocks and they were among the old, beautifully built apartment houses of the Upper West Side.

"Here y'are," the driver said. He had been listening to his radio most of the time and ignored the conversation behind him.

"Come along now," Lawrence said, pushing Jonathan out of the taxi ahead of him. He thrust some bills through the window. The tip would be obscenely large, but he didn't want that nosy driver looking at his face any longer than necessary. His photograph hadn't appeared in any newspaper for several years. But once it had been in every paper and news magazine in the country. And he was afraid of long memories.

"Just along here," Lawrence said, walking quickly west. His hand was around Jonathan's arm.

"I don't understand Dad's wanting me to come up here," Jonathan said. He sounded both angry and afraid and pulled against the man's hold.

"He'll tell you himself in just a minute." Lawrence stopped about halfway along the block in front of a narrow gray stucco house.

Jonathan had a glimpse of the Hudson River seen through the trees of Riverside Park, of a brownstone house next door, where a Siamese cat, like Susan, was in the window, sitting beside a yellow flower in a potted plant. The next moment they were walking up the steps of the apartment house. Lawrence, his hand retaining its hold on Jonathan's arm, smiled down at him. "Any moment now you'll be with your father." Jonathan stared at the doorknob, a leopard's head with a ball in its mouth. He wondered if they were going to use it. But the man inserted his key and the next moment they were in the elevator.

Patrick Tierney burst into his agent's reception area to find Fremantle, Barry and the detective, Mooney, all standing there, looking tense.

"You're sure you didn't show the pictures to anyone?" Mooney was asking Barry.

"I'm sure," Barry said. His eyes slid to Patrick. "Hello, Mr. Tierney. Will you please tell the detective here that you asked me to take those pictures of Jonathan. And I'm sorry about his not . . . about his being missing."

Fremantle turned. "Patrick, for God's sake. This is a hell of a thing! I'm sorry! I'm sure he's going to show up, having decided to take French leave of some kind. But I know how you must feel. Anything at all we can do—just tell us!"

Patrick was fond of Fremantle and knew that he owed him a lot, but for a moment he wanted to throw back, "No, you can't know how I feel!" Because Fremantle, thrice married and busy courting number four, had never had children.

Instead, Patrick said, "Thanks." And to Mooney, "Have you found anything?"

Mooney shook his head. Then he asked, "Did you show your pictures to anyone at all?"

"No. I didn't have anyone to show them to. I used another of the shots to put in a leather traveling frame I have. The rest are in my file drawer." Patrick turned to Barry. "Did you show them to anyone?"

If Patrick had asked that question before the arrival of the detective, Barry knew he would have gladly told him that Cheryl had seen and admired them. But the cop's interest changed everything.

"No, Mr. Tierney, like I told the detective here, I didn't show them to anybody."

"Okay." He paused. "Where you had them developed, would somebody there have seen them or borrowed them?"

"No, like I said, I develop my own."

"Well," Patrick said, "I guess that's that."

"What are you thinking might have happened if he did show the pictures to somebody?" Fremantle asked. He was far from naïve, but long work with contracts and familiarity with the world of words made him prefer to have things spelled out when possible.

Mooney hesitated. He was a compassionate man and didn't, at this point, want to present to Patrick's imagination some of the more frightening things that could happen to an eight-year-old boy. But moving quickly was right now more important than compassion.

"Jonathan is a good-looking boy—an unusually good-looking boy. There are markets for such kids. I'm sure you know that, Mr. Tierney. And there are people whose chief job is to find them, which they do by any means they can, including looking at pictures—anybody's pictures."

"Well," Fremantle said after a silence, "no one has seen Barry's. So I guess Jonathan's all right from that point of view."

Mooney turned to Barry. "Do you have the negatives?"

"Yes."

"I'd like to have them."

"Sure." There was a sick feeling in his stomach. Into his worry for Cheryl a seed of doubt had entered. He refused to acknowledge it. But it did not go away. "I can bring them in tomorrow."

"Why don't I go along with you and pick them up. Where do you live?"

Barry's spirits sank even further. He was ashamed of having anyone see the rathole in the West Fifties which he shared with two other boys. It was a studio containing one pull-out bed and a narrow cot. They had to share the only bureau. But Barry had bought a steel file cabinet which he had placed against the one remaining wall space that wasn't occupied by the sofa bed, the cot, the bureau or the television set. It was in the file cabinet that he kept his photographs and negatives.

"West Fifty-third," he said resignedly.

"May I come along?" Patrick's tone indicated that he did not expect no for an answer.

"If you want to," Mooney said. He turned to Fremantle. "Can I use your phone?"

Fremantle indicated the telephone in the reception area. "Or you can go into any of the offices if you want to be private."

"This is fine." Mooney murmured into the phone for a few minutes, then put down the receiver.

"Any news?" Patrick asked when he was through.

"No." Mooney strove for a reassuring note. "It's pretty early yet, you know. If Jonathan decided to play hooky, which is what it looks like, he's probably not going to go back home before the usual hour."

"But surely he'd guess that when he didn't show at school, the school would be in touch with his family. Where was he when he was supposed to be meeting me?" Patrick hit the table with his open hand.

"How did he sound when you talked to him, Mr. Tierney? Excited? Pleased? Fearful? Resigned?"

"He sounded the way he always sounded when there was a prospect of our getting together. Excited, yes, pleased, yes. Resigned, no, although he ended the conversation quickly because I gather his mother came into the room." He paused. "Have you talked to Mrs. Stanley?"

"No. I called her but there was no answer. I'll try again. We'd better get going after those negatives."

"Yes."

Patrick and Barry went with Mooney in his car to Barry's address. "This whole area used to be called Hell's Kitchen," Mooney said as they got out of the car and he locked it.

Five flights later they were ushered into the small apartment by Barry. The sofa bed was folded, but a swatch of sheet stuck out from behind one of the cushions. The cot, unmade, was shoved in front of it. "Sorry about the mess," he said. Going over to the file cabinet, he unlocked it with a key he took out of his pocket. He rummaged quickly through the folders, then went through them again. After that he paused and stared at the drawer.

"What's the matter?" Patrick asked. Somehow he knew the answer.

"The negatives aren't here," Barry said. "They're gone."

5

MARTHA SAT ON THE HIGH STOOL IN
her kitchen, drinking her sixth cup of coffee. Although she
was an inveterate user of saccharin, dim memories of books
she had read on nutrition made her decide at the fourth cup
to use sugar to counteract the caffeine. The reason she was
sitting on the high stool thrust against the counter instead of
in a more comfortable chair was that, because of her shaking
hands, she couldn't hold the cup. From where she was sitting, she could sip from the cup resting on the counter without attempting to pick it up. Her body was alternately hot
and covered in cold sweat. The demon in her head kept telling
her that if she had a drink—just one drink—she would feel
better and cope better and be better able to help Jonathan.

"Get thee behind me, Satan," she said aloud. She prayed
aloud, too. "Lord, just bring Jonathan back safely and I
won't drink again."

Unfortunately, she had attempted this bargain several times
before, had been given what she asked for, and in due course
picked up a drink.

"I mean it this time," she said aloud, and started to cry. At that moment the telephone rang.

"Have you heard anything?" Megan Stanley asked.

"No," Martha said.

"There was a pause. Then, "Would you like me to come over?"

"No, I'm all right. It's not necessary." Martha knew very well what Megan thought of her. Her answer was dictated by pride and resentment.

"All right. Let me know if I can do anything."

Martha's hand was shaking so badly she could hardly get the receiver back onto the phone. "Moralistic bitch!" she said to herself. And then she forgot to sip from the cup resting on the counter. Instead she picked it up. The cup, shaking in Martha's trembling hand, splashed coffee in every direction, including on her blouse and suit and on Susan, who was lying on the floor a few feet away. Susan gave a wild Siamese cry, sprang up and shook herself.

"I'm sorry," Martha said. "I'm sorry." Sober, she acknowledged to herself that when drinking she had often kicked Susan out of the way. And it was Jonathan's cat. Guilt flooded through her. She slid off the stool and tried to approach Susan. But Susan had learned early not to tangle with Martha. With another cry she sped out of the kitchen.

"I said I'm sorry," Martha cried, running after Susan. But she tripped over a garbage can and went sprawling.

Lying on the floor, she burst into tears and was still lying there when the phone rang again. Getting up was painful, but she moved as quickly as she could and snatched up the receiver.

"Hello?" she cried.

"It's Sarah Jennings. I just called to see if you're all right and whether you'd heard anything."

Martha stared at the wide run in her pantyhose and the scraped skin on her knee. "I haven't heard anything and I haven't had a drink, if that's what you mean."

"That's wonderful!" Sarah said. "Is there anything I can

do? I can't leave the school for several hours, but short of that—"

"Just let me know if you hear from Jonathan or the detective or even my husband—my former husband."

"Of course I will." And then, "Try some broth, it's very soothing to the stomach."

The moment Sarah said that, Martha knew that Sarah was referring to her hangover and she bitterly resented it. "How would you know?" she snapped. She didn't really expect an answer.

"My older brother, David, is a member of AA. When he was newly sober and shaking to pieces he drank quarts of soup, more quarts of sweet tea, and lots of ice cream and candy. Your body loses a lot of sweet when you cut out alcohol. I'll call back later." And she hung up.

"Asshole!" Martha said to herself. Then she put her head in her hands. "I must *not* drink," she said aloud. After a while she looked at her half cup of muddy coffee, picked up her cup and saucer and took them to the sink. They rattled in her hand as she carried them and seemed to fly into the sink of their own accord. The cup broke, splashing more dregs onto Martha's skirt, which was already stained from the previous mishap.

Martha stood and stared at it. Where was Jonathan? What would they do with him? Mental pictures drawn from lurid newspaper and tabloid stories filled her mind. As a sometime writer on a news magazine she had also read her share of police stories of their raids on centers of child pornography and graphic accounts of what child abusers and pornographers did to the children they seduced or kidnapped.

"Oh God, oh God!" she cried, her head down between her arms resting on the drainboard.

The phone rang again. Again, it was Sarah. "Listen, Martha, I just called my brother. He said he thought it would be better—less dangerous—for you if you went into a detox center. He'd be glad to call the one he was in to see if they have a bed."

"I'm not going anywhere away from this house as long as Jonathan might be trying to get in touch with me, or the people who kidnapped him—if they did."

"All right," Sarah said slowly. "I can understand your feeling that way."

"That's hogwash, Sarah. You're not a drunk and you're not a mother. It's impossible for you to understand how I feel. And don't patronize me."

"All right, Martha." Sarah was reining in her temper— not an easy thing to do. "I won't bother you."

"Unless you hear about or from Jonathan," Martha screeched as Sarah slapped the phone down.

It rang again immediately. "Hello," Martha said breathlessly.

"Hi! Found Jon yet?" There was a slur in the words.

"Hello, Katie. No." She added, "You've been drinking."

"You told me to have a drink when you called this morning."

"Well, you've had more than one." A small voice within reminded her that alcohol was the main element in their friendship.

"If that isn't the pot calling the kettle black! What have you done since this morning? Taken the pledge? Gone to AA?"

"Oh shut up!" Martha slammed down the phone.

At the other end Katie replaced the receiver and stared at it angrily. "All right, Mrs. Pure and Holy. If you want to find out about that man I've seen lurking around the street then you're going to have to come off your high horse and apologize." Weaving towards the kitchen she poured herself another vodka on the rocks and took a swallow. "Dry. Very dry," she said. And then, "That'll teach her."

For a moment she thought she should call Martha back anyway and force her to listen to her report on the loitering stranger. But her ego was hurting. When the Tierneys first moved into the apartment in the brownstone three doors down, Katie had called, bringing them a bottle.

But she didn't see much of them at first. In fact, she was convinced they looked down on her. After Patrick left, she saw more of Martha, although not much while she was still working. When she quit (or was fired) Martha had taken to dropping in on Katie. As her drinking grew, so did the friendship. But Katie always had the idea that Martha condescended to her, and she resented it.

It was only in the last hour that she had remembered the man—tall, with a bony face and intense dark eyes under a shock of dark hair. He was, in a weird way, attractive, which was why Katie began to watch for him. She thought about him a lot, which was one reason she was a little hesitant to bring him up. Katie liked men, especially attractive ones. Once, when they had been drinking together, Katie had regaled Martha with some of the romantic tales of her life. Martha, far from sober, had giggled and said, "You seem to go for the wounded-hero type."

Katie felt she was being made fun of, and regretted saying anything about the matter. She had not brought up the subject of men since.

"Bloody snob," she said now. Sinking into her favorite chair, she pushed the On button in the remote control of her television set. Her favorite soap opera was about to start. Mrs. Saintly Tierney could just come hat in hand if she wanted any information from Katie. With another press of her finger she turned up the volume. She liked everything loud. That way it blotted out reality. And anyway, the neighbors weren't home in the middle of the day or—Katie checked her watch—the early afternoon.

The self-service elevator opened and Lawrence and Jonathan got out. There were only two doors in the small foyer. The silence was total.

Fumblingly, Lawrence got out a key and opened one of the doors. "Run on in," he said to Jonathan.

Jonathan hesitated, his fear stronger. "Are you sure Dad's here?"

Lawrence felt panic clawing at him. The walls were thick all right, but that would not prevent the people in the apartment opposite from hearing if Jonathan took it in his head to scream right outside their front door. Then inspiration struck. He put on a performance of studying his watch.

"We got here quicker than I thought. It's still a little before the time when your father said he'd be here. But let's wait inside where we can sit down."

"What time is it?"

"Around noon."

"What time were we supposed to meet Dad?"

"Twelve-thirty. Let's go in."

Jonathan might still have balked if the phone hadn't started to ring in the apartment.

"Come on," Lawrence said. "That might be your father now."

Jonathan ran in and picked up the phone. "Dad?" he said.

A male voice said, "Is Mr. Miller there?"

Jonathan, let down, said to Lawrence, "Are you Mr. Miller?"

Lawrence took up the receiver. "Ben?"

"I called to see if you had the boy yet." The voice at the other end gave a gravelly laugh. "I guess the answer's yes."

"Yes," Lawrence said.

"I want him ready to film when I get there later today. Until then, well, he's yours. But don't lose him."

"I won't."

When Lawrence hung up, Jonathan said, "Dad's not here."

"I told you. He will be soon."

"You said this was his agent's apartment. Will the agent be here, too?"

"Of course. Now, why don't we have some soda. Would you like a Coke?"

"Mom doesn't approve of my drinking Cokes. She said it's bad for my teeth. But I'll take one."

"All right. Why don't you go over and look at the river?

You can see a little of it from the bedroom window. Sometimes sailing ships go past.''

Jonathan wasn't a sailboat enthusiast, but he was liking Lawrence less and less. He even admitted to himself that he was afraid of him. So he'd rather watch boats than hang around the guy. "All right. Where's the bedroom?"

"The one that has the view is through that door." And Lawrence pointed towards the back and right of the apartment. Once he was in there, Lawrence figured, the boy's retreat would be cut off. If worse came to worst Lawrence could lock the bedroom door. And Ben was right. This was an old building. Jonathan could scream his heart out and nobody would hear him. "You look at the boats," he said to Jonathan, "and I'll get the sodas."

When Lawrence came into the bedroom carrying two sodas, Jonathan was staring out the window at the Hudson River. "There aren't any boats," he said crossly. An enormous sense of unease was welling up in him.

"Sometimes there aren't any for a few minutes, but usually one or two come along." Lawrence sipped his gin and tonic, which was more gin than tonic. Generally he preferred drugs to alcohol, but money had been short of late. Once Jonathan had been delivered, there'd be more money. So, much as he hated the thought of having such a short time with Jonathan himself, he felt that his personal needs came first.

"Don't you want your soda?" he asked.

"Sure." Jonathan was busy watching a sailboat and two tugboats that had appeared. Absently he sucked up some of the ice floating at the top of the soda. "What are those things for?" He turned and pointed to three tall standing lights in two corners and against one wall.

"For filming—filming models," Lawrence improvised as casually as he could. "You know, the pictures you've seen in magazines—women modeling new fashions."

"What a funny place to film them," Jonathan said. But he

wasn't really interested. Oddly, he began to feel a little less tense.

Lawrence held his breath. He had been assured that the mild muscle relaxer he had put in the soda would not be detectable. What he would have liked most would be to have time to court the boy, and he had no doubt that he could successfully seduce him. But he wasn't going to be given that. So he felt he was justified in drugging him to make him more physically manageable. As Lawrence now went on talking in a slow, soothing, almost hypnotic way, he watched for the first sign that the drug had taken effect.

"All right," Mooney said, "let's take it from the beginning. Who could have gotten at your files?"

The studio apartment was so small that he and Patrick Tierney and Barry, all standing, occupied what room there was in the middle of the floor.

"I don't know," Barry said for the umpteenth time.

"Were any of your other pictures taken?"

Barry shook his head. "No, I haven't done that many. I think I'd notice."

"Well, look again. And look carefully."

Barry, almost sick with fright, went down on one knee again to look into the single file drawer. Quickly but thoroughly he examined every folder. "Nothing else is missing."

"Why would anyone want to steal them?" Patrick asked. The only answer that made any sense filled him with horror and fear on behalf of his son.

Mooney sat down on the cot. "You said you developed them. Where? You certainly don't have space for a darkroom here."

"I rent one at the photographic institute."

"Couldn't somebody have seen them there?"

"I suppose so."

"Look at me," Mooney said sharply.

Barry jumped and looked up to the taller man.

"I'm going to ask it all over again. Did you show them to anybody?"

Barry, terrified for Cheryl and now terrified for himself, did a fatal thing: he hesitated.

"Okay," Mooney said. "Who was it?"

"My—my girlfriend," Barry said. His own cowardice humiliated him. But he had been badly shaken by finding all the negatives of Jonathan's pictures gone. There was only one person who knew where he kept them—Cheryl. One dull afternoon they had come up here and made love on his lunch hour and he had shown her not only some of his other pictures, but also where he kept the spare set of file keys.

"Name," Mooney said.

"Cheryl."

"Cheryl what?"

"Cheryl Mason."

"Address?"

"I don't know . . . exactly. I mean, I've never been there."

"But you know her phone number."

"Sure. 555-4356."

"Is that office or home?"

"It's the only number I have. If she doesn't answer, somebody—or some service—picks it up."

"Where does she live?"

"In Queens."

"Where in Queens?"

"I dunno. She lives with her family."

"Yeah? And where do you have your loving get-togethers?"

"Here. Nobody's here during the day. Or maybe . . . well, sometimes they aren't here at night."

"Or you pay them to stay away? Right? Where does she work?"

"In an employment agency on West Forty-ninth."

"Have you been there?" Patrick asked.

"No."

"Why did you show them to her?" Patrick's questions were sharp, like a staccato beat.

"I always show her stuff I've done. She's interested."

"Was she more interested in the pictures of Jonathan than in the others?"

"Yes, yes, I guess so."

"What makes you think that?"

"Well . . . she said she wanted to show them to her boss. Something about . . . about kids appearing in commercials, about it being a great opportunity for them."

"And you believed that crap?" Patrick his worst fears about the theft of the pictures realized, lashed out.

Barry winced. Those deep-seated unacknowledged doubts of the past hours were being dragged up to the light. "Look, Cheryl's not that kind of girl. I mean, there are kids on TV. You see them all the time."

"And reputable agencies handle them and won't have them anywhere near the studios without their mothers."

Mooney glanced at Patrick, but there was no point at this moment in pussyfooting around. He looked back at Barry. "Haven't you heard of child pornography?"

"She wouldn't do that," Barry said weakly. But he knew now that was what it was.

Patrick and Mooney stood on the pavement outside Barry's ratty building. Barry himself had fled on foot to the nearest subway to return to his office. He felt bitter and humiliated. Anger within him struggled with a stubborn remnant of loyalty to Cheryl. It was still possible she was innocent.

"Well," Patrick said impatiently, "what're we waiting for? Let's find her."

"What the hell else do you think I'm trying to do?"

"I mean let's go over to that address on West Forty-ninth Street."

"Okay."

They went to where Mooney's car was parked. Inside, he

picked up a phone and dialed. Then he said, "Get me anything you have on one Cheryl Mason. Call me back."

The answer came before they reached the block between Eighth and Ninth Avenues. The phone buzzed. Mooney picked it up, listened, then said, "Thanks." He put the receiver down. "Nothing," he said.

When the car pulled up in front of the address Barry had given them they both stared at the brownstone, which contained, on ground level, a grocery store. Before Mooney could say anything Patrick got out of the car and strode up the brownstone steps. Mooney followed.

Patrick examined the bells in the dirty outer lobby. Most of them had no names beside them. Impatiently, he pushed one marked SUPER.

"There's not going to be any super," Mooney said.

"What makes you so sure?"

"Places like this don't have resident supers. The guy who owns this isn't going to waste a perfectly good apartment on somebody's he's going to have to pay—or even house rent-free."

"Doesn't he have to have somebody in charge of the property and maintenance?"

"Maintenance is a word owners of dumps like this have never heard of. He probably comes around and looks at it himself from time to time, or somebody does it for him. Let's try something else." Methodically he pushed each bell, waiting a second to see if anybody answered. Finally a female voice squawked through the box. "Whad'ya want?"

"Police," Mooney said laconically.

"The door's open anyway."

Patrick pushed the inner door and it flew open.

Mooney pushed the same bell again.

"Yeah?"

"Do you know anything about an employment agency in this building?"

"Here? Are you kidding?"

"Well," Mooney said to Patrick, "how do you feel about another five flights?"

They went straight up. By the time they got to the top, Mooney was puffing. Methodically, they started ringing bells. There were no signs announcing an employment agency. Most of the time the doorbells produced no answer. When it was apparent from listening that somebody was inside, Mooney kept on knocking until the door was finally opened. Several disgruntled citizens in various states of undress came to the door. No one had ever heard either of an employment agency or of a woman named Cheryl Mason until someone on the second floor, a thick-tongued man in undershorts and nothing else, said something that sounded like, "She used to live here," prior to passing out before their eyes and falling hard on the splintered wooden floor.

"Let's get him up," Mooney said.

They pushed their way in.

"Pew!" Patrick wrinkled his nose.

The stench—a combination of unwashed bodies and a broken toilet—was overwhelming. They walked back through the railroad apartment. In each room was a bed and nothing else. Needles were everywhere.

"We'll put him here for the time being," Mooney said, indicating the bed in the first room.

"Shouldn't we send for an ambulance?"

"That's what I'm intending. But I don't see a phone here, do you? I'll have to send for one from the car." They finished ringing bells on that floor, on the ground floor and in the basement. Nobody else who answered had heard of an employment agency or Cheryl Mason.

Finally they went down the stoop and over to the curb. Mooney slid into his car, reached for the phone and called for an ambulance. When he'd done that he dialed again and asked, "Any news of Jonathan Tierney?" After a minute he looked out to where Patrick was standing. "No news," he said. Then he dialed the school and asked for Sarah Jennings. When he had spoken to her for half a minute, he again looked out at Patrick. "She hasn't heard anything either. Do you want to call Mrs. Tierney or shall I?"

"You call her. That'll upset her less."

After he'd hung up, Mooney said, "No news, but she sounds terrible."

"You mean drunk?"

"No. Not drunk. Terrible."

Jonathan, Lawrence thought, was taking an unconsciona- bly long time to show any effects of the pill in his soda. "Drink your soda, Jonathan," he said.

"I don't like it," Jonathan said. "How much longer are we going to wait before Dad gets here?"

"He must have been held up. Now, drink your soda. He'll be here in no time at all."

"I've got to go to the bathroom," Jonathan said. He turned and was out of the room before Lawrence knew it.

"Come back here!" Lawrence yelled.

The phone rang. Jonathan headed towards the front door of the apartment, but Lawrence cut him off. "You're not leaving here."

"You're not a friend of Dad's. He wouldn't have a friend like you." Memories of instruction by teachers at school, even by his mother on one of the occasions when she was sober, occurred to him. *If any man gets hold of you, or tries to take you anywhere, scream, scream as loud as you can and as long as you can. Somebody may hear you.*

So as he ran, Jonathan screamed and yelled as loud as he could. "Help! Help!"

The phone was still ringing. Lawrence, who had run straight for the apartment's front door to stop Jonathan, was now trying to get hold of him. But Jonathan was as slippery as an eel. He darted around furniture. Finally he flew into another bedroom and locked the door from inside with a bolt under the knob.

Lawrence pounded on the door, then went to answer the

phone. Jonathan saw there was an extension on the night table beside the bed.

Modeling his action on what he had seen in the movies and on television, he lifted the receiver as quietly as he could.

"What's that?" a man's voice said.

"Nothing," Lawrence replied.

Jonathan wondered why Lawrence didn't tell the man on the phone the truth, that it was the click of the bedroom telephone extension. But he was enlightened a moment later.

The man said, "Everything all right with the kid?"

"Fine. We're getting along fine."

"Okay. I want him bright and in good condition for the filming tonight. I'm bringing up a new camera. I'll be there around seven. Don't scare the kid too much. He's got to be able to do his part. After that, you can scare him all you want."

Jonathan replaced the phone and looked around him. This was a far bigger bedroom than the other. In the corners were more lights on stands. Cables trailed over the floor. What looked like a television camera was in one corner.

Jonathan was neither stupid nor unimaginative. He knew what they were for and why he was here. Cold fear ran through him. He desperately wanted his father. But his father was somehow mixed up with this man. How else would he have known Jonathan was waiting in the doughnut shop for him? Unless, of course, he'd just seen him and pretended to be a friend of his father's.

Jonathan tried to calm his panic and remember everything Lawrence had said about his father. He knew his father was a writer, or was that from something he, Jonathan, had told him? His mind was in a whirl. Who could be trusted? Jonathan lay down on the bed, trying to shut out the sounds of Lawrence pounding on the door. After a while the pounding stopped.

Curious. Jonathan found himself thinking about his mother. Not the blowsy woman who lately was so seldom sober, but the woman he remembered when the two of them had gone to a street fair and eaten knishes and hot dogs, the woman who used to read to him and play with him and would comfort him when he had nightmares, turning on the light, sitting on the bed and putting her arm around him, saying, "It's all right, Jonathan. It's only a dream, darling, just a bump in the night." Thinking about it brought a sense of safety. He knew that the safety wasn't real, that it didn't change anything about the man on the other side of the door. But it made him feel better just the same. "It's only a bump in the night," he said to himself quietly.

Then the pounding started again.

Jonathan sat up. His limbs felt a little heavy. Fear went through him once more. He remembered the soda. But he'd only sucked that one piece of ice. Maybe two. He had stood and stared out the window, holding the soda, the ice in his mouth, while the man talked and talked and talked. But he hadn't drunk from the soda. I didn't drink from it, he reassured himself.

"Jonathan," the man called, "let me in this minute. I mean you no harm. You'll like some of the games I'll teach you. Let me in."

Jonathan stood there, saying nothing. Then abruptly the pounding stopped. Jonathan found that more frightening than the noise. That meant the man was probably going to get tools to force the door open, or to get someone to help him, someone who wouldn't believe Jonathan no matter what he said.

He looked around frantically. Curtains lined the windows, but heavy as they were, they wouldn't hide him. He went to the window and looked out. Maybe someone from another window would see him or, if he opened the window, would hear him. But the windows wouldn't budge. Jonathan didn't know whether they were simply stuck or were sealed.

There was another sound at the door. Jonathan whirled around. Whoever was on the other side was doing something to the doorknob. There was an odd clicking, scraping sound. Jonathan glanced quickly over the room. Besides the door to the hall, there were two other doors. One, which was open, led to the bathroom. The other was to a closet. Jonathan ran over to the closet and yanked open the door. There were all kinds of strange clothes inside—net things that stuck out, dresses, pants. But Jonathan didn't have time to examine them. He was about to plunge through the clothes to hide behind them, when he noticed how deep the shelves were above the clothing. Boxes of all sizes were on them. He'd do better up there behind the boxes, he decided.

Quickly he hung on to the bottom shelf, then pulled himself up. Getting from there to the top shelf was easy. Pushing the various boxes to the front of the shelf, he lay down behind them.

Lying there, he found himself staring up at the ceiling paper. The design of the paper seemed to consist of a dizzying pattern of squares. One large square near the corner seemed to have thicker lines than the others. He put his hand up and felt it with his fingers and realized the lines were cracks. His heart started to beat faster. Placing his hands against the square, he pushed up. It moved at one corner. He pushed harder. The whole trapdoor lifted, making a slight noise. He lay quiet, listening. But all he could hear was the same clicking, scratching sound at the bedroom door. Getting his sneakered feet under him, he stood up. His head and shoulders seemed to be in a small attic. Around him were more boxes and a big trunk. Gripping the sides of the square hole, he jumped, pulling himself up and hauling himself inside. Then, as quietly as he could, he fitted the door back and lay on it, his heart beating.

Cheryl, unaware of the man who had been following her at a safe distance since she left the restaurant, made her way back to her place of work, which was not the fictitious employment agency whose address she had made up on the spur of the moment, but the room above the film-developing studio between Seventh Avenue and Broadway.

"How's the boy wonder?" Ben asked when she stepped from the elevator into the second floor.

"From Nowheresville. I tried to get the idea across of his taking pictures of kids, in the park or on the street, you know, for commercials, but he didn't bite."

"Maybe he can be made to."

"Yeah? How?"

"Leak the fact that he took the pictures he gave you to the police and tell them that they're being used for porn movies. The cops aren't going to swallow that he didn't know. We'd tell him that if he did a few more pictures for us, then we'd tell the cops that we made a mistake, that he was innocent."

Cheryl thought about it. She had been working since she was sixteen, first as a hooker, then as a model for some of the seedier porn magazines and, later, in films. She had learned that what mattered was getting paid, and how and for what and through whom the money came mattered little. She worked for people who meant what they said and saw that those who got in their way or didn't cooperate were punished. None of this had she ever questioned. She had lied to Barry about living in Queens with her family. Her jobs had paid her way out of the home where, since she was twelve, her father had assaulted her physically and verbally. When he'd had more than three drinks he abused her sexually, and her mother was always too weak and too frightened to help. She now lived in a small apartment in Tribeca, the newly gentrified area below SoHo. She had let Barry pick her up in a disco. He was young and she found his small-town innocence oddly attractive. It was only when he showed her the photographs of Jonathan that she saw he might have other uses. But, having hesitated at little in her life when it promised profit, she found herself unwilling now to blackmail Barry. Unfortunately, in her enthusiasm over his pictures of Jonathan, she had shown them to her boss, and since then his interest in Barry and his photographs was greater than her own.

"Let me see what I can do," she said, and congratulated herself that she had had the foresight to steal Barry's negatives one afternoon when he and his roommates were at work and that she had not make the mistake of telling her boss Barry's full name or his address.

When she left the studio off Broadway she got on a subway to go downtown to her apartment. She got out at Canal and then started walking north and west. The man caught up with her when she was in an alley between Greene and West Broadway.

"Hello, Cheryl," he said.

She turned quickly. "Hi, Leo." Her heart started beating. "Long time no see."

Leo had been useful at one point in her life. He had, in fact, served as her pimp. Then he introduced her to Ben, who saw her further possibilities. Through Ben she found her way into porn films and decided there were better methods of making a living than on her back. Leo hadn't been happy with her decision. For one thing, it was a bad example for his other girls. He told her to come back or she might find herself unable to pursue any career at all. Cheryl, riding high, told him he was a loser and to get lost. Afterwards, she remembered various girls he had cut up and, belatedly, felt afraid. But her courage returned when a slight professional miscalculation on his part had landed him in jail. She figured that by the time he came out she'd be pursuing her career in California. He had indeed spent a few years behind bars, where his grievance against Cheryl had grown ugly. But he was showing up a little bit earlier than she had bargained for. He didn't say anything, but something about the silence and the way he stood filled her with terror for her life.

She moistened her lips. "Leo—"

The silencer muffled the shots that went into her, one in her heart, one in the middle of her forehead.

Leo stood looking down at her, making sure she was dead. Stooping, he took her bag, removed all identification from it, putting it in his pocket, and threw the bag back down again. Then he walked to the end of the alley and melted into the usual traffic on West Broadway.

6

AT THE END OF HER FAVORITE SOAP opera, Katie Leonard was in a repentant mood. Vodka had eased her early morning grumpiness. On the other hand, the particular sequence she had been watching had been about the terrible destruction alcohol can cause in a home. Also, the face of the man who had been loitering had appeared again and again between her and the television screen, and at the end of the hour the face was less attractive than she had thought. Impulsively, she picked up the phone and dialed Martha.

It was picked up on the first ring. "Hello?"

Katie could tell that Martha had been poised, hoping and waiting for news about Jonathan. Quickly Katie said, "It's me, Katie. Listen, there's something I want to tell you, although it may mean nothing."

"Oh!" Martha's letdown was obvious, but Katie refused at this point to be deflected. "I should have thought of it sooner, but I only remembered, after we talked, that there was a man standing around outside today and yesterday. I noticed him because . . . well, I just did.''

"What man?'' Martha said sharply.

"I just told you. A man. I don't know who he was. He sort of loitered across the street and strolled back and forth.''

"Why didn't you tell me this sooner?''

"Look,'' Katie said, her minimal supply of understanding depleted, "you want me to tell you about him or you want to have a fight?''

Martha took hold of herself. "Sorry. Let's begin at the beginning. When did you first notice this man?''

"I don't know. I'm not sure. It could have been a couple of days ago, because when I saw him I had the odd feeling that I'd seen him before. So I decided I must have seen him at one of the street parties around here or something. Then I saw him yesterday, off and on. And then this morning.''

Martha put a shaking hand to her forehead and pushed back her hair. Her headache was like a drum beating inside her skull, and nausea gripped her stomach. "You're about three doors down from me, Katie,'' she said. "Help me to visualize this. Was he more in front of my house than yours? Did he walk around? Did he just stand still?''

Katie started to enjoy herself. "He stood for a while more or less on the sidewalk outside your building. Then he strolled away for a while, I guess in the opposite direction away from me. Then when I glanced out again he was coming back towards me again.''

Martha fought back her physical misery and tried to summon recently unused faculties. You're a reporter, she told herself silently. Once a reporter, always a reporter. No matter what.

"Katie,'' she said, as calmly as she could, "can you tell me what it was about the man that made you notice him? I mean, I realize that he was standing there and coming back and forth. But was there anything else?''

Katie was silent for a few minutes, then, "Just this vague feeling that I'd seen him somewhere.''

"Can you describe him? Come on, you're an artist!" It was flattery but it was also true. Before she acquired her handsome alimony, Katie Leonard had done some interesting pencil sketches of notable people. Lately she hadn't done any. But anything was worth a try. "Do you think," Martha said, "you could draw his face for me?"

"Sure. It was a good-looking face. Well, maybe not good-looking, but interesting. Shall I come over there?"

"Please, Katie, do. I don't want to leave the phone."

For the first time in rather a long period, Katie felt wanted and important. "Of course. I'll get my stuff and come along."

A few minutes later she came up the front steps with a large sketch tablet under her arm and some charcoal pieces in her hand.

Martha, who had been watching for her, buzzed her in and waited for her at the apartment door.

It was the first time Katie had seen Martha in a few days and she found the other woman's appearance shocking. She was used to the bloated stomach and the perpetually flushed face. But Martha's skin now seemed a greasy white, with a film that appeared to come from sweat on the forehead and around the mouth. Martha was smoking, and the hand that held the cigarette shook and jerked as she raised the cigarette to her lips.

"You need a drink," Katie said, meaning the best.

"No!" Martha almost shouted. More quietly she said, "I don't want to talk about it. Draw the man's face, Katie. At least we'll have something to go to the police with."

Katie had a whole array of reasons stopping drinking so abruptly could do more harm than good. She decided to give voice to at least one of them. "You could have a convulsion, stopping cold turkey like that."

"Katie, please! I know what I have to do."

Katie shrugged. She'd done her part. "All right. Let me sit down."

Katie, whose talent had always been for the lightning

sketch, drew a few lines. A rather distant likeness of Law-rence's face leaped onto the page. "Do you recognize him?" she asked Martha.

Martha stared at the face. She had seen that face before somewhere, but she couldn't remember where. The memory was neither clear nor strong. "I'm going to call Sergeant Mooney," she said, and went towards the phone.

But Mooney wasn't there. The officer who answered said he'd tell the sergeant next time he called in, and added, "Why don't you bring the drawing here. Maybe somebody here will recognize it."

Martha reported her conversation to Katie. "But I can't leave here," she finished. "Jonathan might try to reach me."

"Do you want me to go to the precinct?" Katie asked.

Martha didn't have too much faith that the police would take Katie seriously. She wasn't drunk, but to any trained eye she wasn't entirely sober. And men, workingmen, had, in Martha's opinion, a tendency to discount whatever was said by an overweight middle-aged woman. She'd once written an article on the subject, documenting the fact that middle-aged women in a man's world were inclined to be slighted; fat middle-aged women were especially slightable. And Katie, billowing around in her muumuu, was both. When you added a strong smell of liquor coming out of the mouth . . . But what else was there to do?

"Okay, Katie, I'll give you the money to take a cab."

"I can pay for it myself. It's my contribution."

"All right. Thanks. Call me from there if there's any news at all or if anybody there recognizes him. Okay?"

Stephen Morgan's father, Albion Morgan, decided to pick up his son from school that afternoon. His last class ended at two o'clock, which meant that he could take the subway at 116th Street and Broadway in Manhattan, change to the express at Ninety-sixth and be in Borough Hall in Brooklyn Heights by three.

Happily he locked his office door, walked rapidly across

the Columbia campus and dived into the subway. His luck held, because a train came along shortly and there was an express waiting across the platform for him at Ninety-sixth. Once on that, he opened his morning paper and devoted himself to the news of the day. In his more radical days, reading the daily paper was a test of how to contain his indignation and rage at Establishment indifference to the crying needs of social justice. But in the past few years he was able to peruse the paper without exploding or wanting to join the most recent revolution.

"Middle-aged complacency," his wife, in one of her more acerbic moments, had called it.

Maybe, he thought now, turning the sheet. But deep in his heart he knew it had something to do with his son, Stephen. For a man who had been less than enthusiastic about the idea of marriage, and had stated flatly that he did not intend to become a parent, he had turned into a besotted father, going to the lengths of arranging his classes so that he could meet his son after school at least twice a week. Those walks home from school, punctuated by a stop at the pizza or ice cream parlor, had become for him what charging the barricades had once been: his greatest satisfaction in life.

When he got out of the train he bounded up the steps of the Borough Hall station, walked rapidly to the school and congratulated himself that he had reached there at exactly the right time.

He was a little annoyed to see Stephen come out with Marguerite Stanley, the two of them talking, or rather, Morgan observed morosely, Marguerite talking and Stephen listening. She was a pushy, unattractive child, he thought, and why Stephen chose her as his best friend, he didn't know. Then he amended that. It was probably not his doing, but Marguerite's. Whatever. The fact was that she and Stephen were close buddies and that meant that he had to invite her along.

"Hi, Stephen!" he said as the two approached.

Stephen's face lit up. "Hi, Dad!"

"Hi, Mr. Morgan," Marguerite said.

"Hello, Marguerite," Morgan said. He turned towards Stephen. "How about some ice cream or some pizza?"

Speaking at the same time, Stephen said, "Pizza," and Marguerite said, "Ice cream."

"Pizza it is. Let's go to the place on Montague."

As they turned towards Montague Street Stephen burst out, "Dad, Jonathan's not in school and everybody's looking for him and the teachers were asking Marguerite and me and we said Jonathan was with his father. I mean," Stephen went on desperately, "that's what you said the other night. When you were talking to Ma in the kitchen."

"I said he was at an animal shelter," Marguerite said.

Morgan stopped in the middle of the sidewalk. "Let me get this straight. Jonathan didn't show up in school today?"

"That's right," Stephen said. "And Miss Babson asked if anybody knew where he was." He paused.

"And you said?"

"Well, I forgot you told Ma not to say anything." Stephen adored his father, but he was also a little afraid of him.

"So what did you tell her?"

"It wasn't his fault, Mr. Morgan," Marguerite loyally joined in. "He sort of likes Miss Babson and—"

"I'm not asking you, Marguerite," Morgan snapped. Why couldn't the child shut up? "What did you say, Stephen?"

Stephen gathered his courage. "I said Jonathan was with Mr. Tierney."

"Oh Christ! Since you were listening to our conversation, you heard your mother and me agree how important it was that Jonathan's father not do anything foolish to louse up his chances of getting custody, didn't you?"

"Yes." Stephen stared at his toes.

Morgan's spurt of temper peaked. "All right. It's okay, but next time ask me before you get entangled in a custody suit."

"Yes," Stephen said.

Marguerite took his hand.

For a moment Stephen was grateful for the gesture of solidarity. Then he pushed her hand away. His father would consider that a weakness.

Morgan wished that he and Stephen were alone. But short of asking Marguerite to leave them, there was nothing he could do about it now. Besides, there was the matter of Jonathan.

"Did anyone get in touch with his mother?"

Stephen didn't answer for a moment. No one had actually said she'd called Martha Tierney. On the other hand, the fact that Jonathan's mother had come to the school was well broadcast over the school grapevine. And then there was the policeman who'd questioned them. "Well, they must have. I mean, even before they called the policeman."

"They called the police?"

"Yes."

"My God, he really is missing. Does his father know?"

"He's got to," Marguerite said. "He was at the school, but we didn't see him."

"Well, I hope to God your saying Jonathan might be with his father won't ruin his father's custody plans." Morgan saw his son's fallen face. "It's okay. You didn't realize the seriousness. Let's get to the pizza place. They may have a pay phone there."

Police Officer Claude Johnson looked at the charcoal sketch brought by Katie Leonard. "I don't recognize it," he said.

"Don't you have pictures of criminals, sex offenders, that you could maybe compare it to?"

"Did you show it to Mrs. Tierney?"

"Of course. She told me to bring it here. She's a close friend."

That figures, Johnson thought. According to community gossip they were both drunks. The alcohol fumes coming across from Katie, as she leaned forward and talked, were powerful. Johnson, a conscientious officer, tried not to be prejudiced. But he was an elder in his African Methodist Church and it was hard not to class a drunken woman with the other abominations mentioned in the Bible. If she had been black, he would have been even more intolerant, because added to drunkenness would be the charge of bringing disgrace on her already oppressed people. But Katie was white. He glanced at the heavy woman. Under her raincoat she had on some kind of shapeless garment. Her hair, he noted, was stove black with no highlights. Dyed, he thought. His wife wore her hair natural, which was the way he liked and approved.

"You can look at some pictures," he said. "I'll get out one of the books."

"All right." Then she added, "I'm an artist, you know, so I have a good eye for resemblances."

And for the liquor label, Johnson thought as he went to get the book containing several years' worth of criminals. Irritated, he didn't check the front of the book he brought back, or he would have realized it was photographs of men booked for assault and armed robbery.

Jonathan, lying flat, could hear the voices underneath.

"I tell you, he was in the room. He'd locked himself in."

That was the voice of the man who had kidnapped him. Jonathan knew that as long as he lived he would recognize it. In some ways it was a voice, or an accent, that reminded him of some of the prissier teachers at school. Then there was another voice.

"Yeah? Well, where's he now?"

"I don't know. Perhaps—"

"Perhaps what?" The coarse-voiced man spoke in mincing tones, obviously mocking the other man.

"Perhaps he unlocked the door while I was in the kitchen looking for a screwdriver so I could break the lock. And then got out of the apartment."

"Was the door unlocked when you came back from the kitchen?"

"I'm—I'm not sure." He had spent some time looking for the heavy screwdriver, then came back, and, without trying the door again, jammed the tool into the lock between the door and the doorjamb and pushed and twisted until the door sprang open.

"You mean to tell me you think the kid unlocked the door to get out and then took the time to lock the door behind him?"

"He's very bright."

"If he's that bright, he'd run like hell! Look, you say you don't know whether the door was locked or unlocked when you came back with the screwdriver."

Lawrence hesitated. "I assumed it was locked. I didn't try it. I'm sure he's still here."

"Okay, where? The door's open, the room's empty. Did you look in the closet?"

"Of course. And he's not there."

"Then he's gone. And if he got out it's your tail that's gonna be in a meat grinder. He's never seen me. But he's sure as hell seen you, and if he gets to the cops, then they're going to have you, because they've got your picture from ten years ago."

Lawrence was sweating with fear. "I can't see how he did it, though."

"Oh, you can't! You wanna have another look around? We've only looked twice." The voice was elaborately sarcastic. "If I was you I'd be thinking about getting out of here. He's gone. You're not going to get him back."

"He's not gone." Lawrence's syllables got even more precise. "He couldn't have got out without my hearing. I'm going to have another look around."

"You do what you want. I'm going."

"I don't know why you're here anyway. You said the filming would be tonight."

"I just wanted to make sure everything was okay. You sounded funny, like there was trouble. And I was right. The kid's gone. And I'm not happy about the idea that he may bring the cops back here.''

''He's not going to bring the cops back here because he hasn't escaped.''

''Fine. Find him! I'll watch.''

Patrick was back in his sublet flat again, checking the answering machine to see if he'd had any calls. He had altered the announcement on the tape to identify himself as the current occupant and to urge callers to leave names and phone numbers. But now there was no blinking light to warn of waiting messages.

He found he couldn't sit down. Nervously he turned on the television to an all-news program and realized he was half waiting to hear an announcement of his son's disappearance.

Quickly he glanced at his watch. Three-thirty. Was it only—he did some calculation—eight hours since Jonathan had left home? Home? He pulled his mind away from Martha, where it had a tendency to settle. But to stop himself from angrily blaming her was almost more than he could manage. He decided suddenly that he would write down everything he knew or had heard about where Jonathan had been or was believed to have been since he left home.

Sitting down at the desk, he pulled a yellow lined pad towards him and got out a felt-tip pen.

After a moment he wrote in the margin,

7:30—Left home
7:30–7:35—Went to Megan Stanley's to see kittens.
7:55—Left Stanley's to go to doughnut shop to meet ''nice man.''

At that point, sickened by all the implications in those last two words, Patrick set down his pen and put his head in his hands.

* * *

"How's Simpson?" Marguerite asked her aunt. Although Simpson had looked normal to her that morning, she knew her Aunt Megan was upset that Simpson had seemed indifferent to his breakfast and had had an attack of coughing.

"Fine, thank God, or at least mostly fine. Dr. Buckner said he had a slight cold, that's all."

"So you took him to the vet after all."

"Of course. Didn't I say I was going to?"

"You were making up your mind when I left."

"Jonathan came by after you'd gone." The discomfort that had underlain everything else that morning surfaced. "When he left he said he was going to meet a friend at the doughnut shop."

"What friend?"

"He said he was a nice man—a friend of his father's."

"Aunt Megan, Jonathan's missing. He's not at school and everybody's looking for him."

"Oh my God!" Then he never got to school. The guilt that had been nibbling at her consciousness now thrust aside every other feeling. "I knew I should have called from the vet's. Tell me what happened at school."

"Stephen and I got sent for by the headmistress and a policeman questioned us. People said Jonathan's father was there, though I didn't see him."

"What did they say happened?"

"Jonathan was supposed to meet his father at the doughnut shop on Court Street. But he never showed up."

"Then why did he say it was a friend of his father's? I don't understand that."

"Stephen said it was supposed to be a secret that he was going to be with his father."

"What a mess! But I told him the place on Court Street was closed, so he probably went around the corner to the new one on Atlantic Avenue. I wonder if it makes any difference."

"What do you mean, Aunt Megan?"

"Well, do you think it would, well, help in finding Jonathan if I told someone that?"

"I dunno. Maybe so."

"I've told you, Marguerite, not to be sloppy in your speech. It's 'I don't know.' Not 'I dunno.' "

Old cow, Marguerite thought.

"I don't see any face that looks anything like the man outside my house," Katie Leonard said to Officer Johnson.

One of the officers who had just walked in looked carelessly at the book in front of Katie. "You been in an armed robbery attack, Miss?"

"No. I'm trying to find a—a possible sex pervert who loitered in our neighborhood this morning. You know that Jonathan Tierney, a neighborhood boy, is missing. So I think anyone who was hanging around would be important."

Johnson walked over, looked at the book, glanced at the cover, and said, "Sorry. I guess I got out the wrong book." He went back and got another of the books and took it to Katie. "Here you are."

Katie felt deflated and angry. "I shouldn't think it'd be hard to discover the difference between armed robbery and sexual perversion."

Martha waited for Katie to come back from the precinct. Her hope of anyone there recognizing the sketch was almost zero, yet it was something, however small, that gave her the feeling that an effort of her own to find Jonathan was being set in motion.

This reminded her of Sergeant Mooney. It had been about an hour since he had called. Intellectually she knew that if there were anything new at all he would phone her. But intellectuality had little to do with how she felt. And then there was her physical misery to deal with. Her headache still beat inside her head like tomtoms, nausea kept her from wanting to eat anything, and the fact that she hadn't eaten much since the day before was making her giddy. As though the word had produced the effect, she suddenly felt her head spin and she clutched the kitchen counter. The room around her seemed to turn, head over tail, like an airplane. Her stomach obediently rose, and she wondered for a moment if she were going to go through another period of retching, as she had the previous night. Sweat sprang out on her face.

Straight across the dining room, well within her sight, were the bottles of liquor. She could feel herself unscrewing one of the tops, pouring some into a glass, and drinking, drinking, drinking, with the blissful sense of reality being deferred.

After all, her other self argued, you're not doing Jonathan any good by not drinking, and you'll be better able to think on his behalf. You'll— She didn't know at what point she had let go the counter and was walking across the carpet to the cabinet where the golden and white liquors were kept, her own fruits of the Hesperides. . . .

She had her hand on top of one of the bottles.

"No, no, no," she cried. "No!" She stood up and flung the bottle across the dining area, across the counter to the kitchen in the general direction of the sink. It curved and arced, almost in slow motion. When it hit, it hit the side of the sink with an almighty crash.

She stood there and cried, smelling the liquor fumes as they wafted over to her.

Then she got the mop, a pan and a brush, and went to work cleaning it up.

The trouble was, when she finally stood up, the dizziness came back. She sat down beside the counter. The phone rang.

It was Patrick.

"Heard anything?" he asked.

"No."

"Mooney and I've been in Hell's Kitchen trying to track down some nonexistent employment agency where Barry Pinkus's girlfriend was supposed to have worked."

"Who's Barry Pinkus?"

"Barry's the kid who took those pictures for me, the ones of Jonathan." He waited for her to make some crack about the pictures again, but she didn't.

She was watching her shaking right hand as the blood flowed from it. In brushing up one of the glass shards of the bottle she had flipped it right into her palm, point first. All she said was, "What's Barry's girlfriend got to do with it?"

At this point Patrick was sorry he had mentioned anything about Cheryl. If Martha suspected that Cheryl had been involved in some kiddie-porn ring, it would obliterate whatever control she had. Patrick could almost hear her screaming abuses over what he, in his stupid carelessness, had let their son in for.

"It was just a question of tracking down anyone who's seen the photos. I don't suppose there's anything going on at your end," he finished, without much hope.

"Not much. Katie Leonard insists there was a man hanging around the street here for the last couple of days. She came over and drew a sketch of him."

"I'm surprised she was sober enough to do that." He held his breath, waiting for Martha to launch her attack on his nasty tongue. But she didn't.

"Yes, well, she can still draw. The funny thing is, I have a vague feeling I've seen that face before, but I can't track it down. Or maybe it's just her drawing. Anyway, she's over at the precinct showing it to the cops there. Perhaps they can recognize it."

Patrick paused. "I think I'll go over and look at it myself. I can ask the phone company to forward any calls about Jonathan. They'll do that, I think."

"They will?"

"Sure, if there's a good reason. Why?"

"Because I've been sure I had to stay here myself, in case Jonathan should call. Or anyone else."

"You don't have to go to the precinct. You've already seen the picture. You said you partly recognized it."

"It's just a vague feeling. I can't seem to pin it down."

"You sound funny. You okay?" His deep anger at her prevented him from feeling any concern. On the other hand, she did sound odd.

"Yes." She hesitated, then burst out, "I haven't had a drink today."

"I wonder how long that'll last." The words were out of Patrick's mouth before he was aware even of thinking of them. "I'm sorry," he said. "I didn't mean quite to say that."

"You don't have any scruples about kicking people when they're down, do you?"

"If you're down it's because you didn't look after your son properly. You can't pin that on somebody else."

She hung up.

He called her back right away, but she let her answering tape reply for her. After the beep he said stiffly, "I'm sorry."

Lying flat on the trapdoor above the closet, Jonathan heard Lawrence rummaging around the room immediately outside the closet. Then there was quiet, although a sound came up every now and then, indicating there were still people in the apartment.

Jonathan prayed, Please don't let them find me. Please.

He took a breath. And started to sneeze.

7

JONATHAN LAY RIGID, HIS HAND OVER his face, his finger pressing under his nose to prevent the sneeze from bursting out.

In the biggest room of the apartment, Lawrence was busy flinging open the doors of a large sideboard.

"You're nuts," his companion said. "That bureau is where we store some of the films."

"He could have hidden in here. He's slight enough."

But there was nothing but boxes and boxes of tapes.

"Come on. We don't have any more time to bother about that kid. He's back home by now, trying to tell the cops where this place is. I'm going to get the hell out, and you'd better too, if you have any brains, which I doubt."

"If the cops come here, is there anything to link us to this place?"

"No. They'll get some pretty good porn movies, but there's nothing on them to link us. Come on. My car's on the Drive. I'll give you a lift." He was convinced by now that Lawrence was more hazard than asset. When he first encountered Lawrence he sounded as if he'd be a good customer, and further, he seemed to have a successful line to the kid in the pictures—a kid who had the looks to go far in the films the man planned. But now the kid was gone, there was some danger that he could remember enough to get the police back here, and this screwball wanted to stay and take the place apart when it was perfectly obvious that the boy— no dummy—had split.

Trapped by rage and frustration, Lawrence didn't say anything for a moment. He had been stalking Jonathan now for nearly a week. And for days before that he had the photographs of the exquisite boy to look at and touch while he worked out various plans to accost him and get him away from his neighborhood.

His companion, Ben Nicolaides, who was also the proprietor of the second-floor establishment off Broadway, had first shown him the pictures, the ones that Cheryl had brought back after a lunch with Barry Pinkus.

Ben had known that not much mileage could be derived from the photographs by themselves unless the boy could be got hold of and induced to act in films. By showing the prints to Lawrence and feeding him the details as to where Jonathan lived and went to school, Ben thought he might kill two birds with one stone. He could, of course, have dispatched one of the other men he knew whom he had used before in the acquisition and seduction of children. But this eager, intellectual-looking man was far better for the purpose. From everything Ben had been able to gather from Cheryl about the boy—his father's being a writer and so on—he'd be more likely to cotton to a man who talked in the same way. Or so Ben argued to himself.

So Lawrence had gone to Brooklyn Heights and strolled around the streets where Jonathan lived and went to school. He was convinced that no one had noticed anything odd in his behavior, but he had not found an opportunity to talk to Jonathan until the morning he had followed Jonathan to Megan Stanley's house and from there to the doughnut shop on

Atlantic Avenue. He knew the boy's father was a writer and that he had a literary agent. That much Ben had got from Cheryl and had passed on to Lawrence. From there he winged it and had done it, he convinced himself, remarkably successfully—until he had managed to break the lock on the bedroom door and burst it open, only to find Jonathan gone.

"He could *not* have gone out," he said. "Look, you go on. I'm going to wait. I know he's here somewhere."

"And I think you're crazy. What's more, you could blow the thing if the cops come."

"I won't blow anything."

"And don't expect any help."

"I won't."

He waited until the man had left. Then Lawrence raised his voice. "I know you're here somewhere, Jonathan. And I'm going to find you."

The old sense of power filled him. For so long he'd been good—obeying the stupid doctors, taking the medicine that slowed him down, stripped him of his visions, tied him to the earth.

Now, as he always knew when he was allowed to be himself, when a blind, stupid and inhibited society was not dictating the terms of his freedom, now he could see the truth: the truth was himself and the boy. Glorious images filled his mind. Together they would be invincible. "I'm going to find you," he cried again, a clarion call to the magic future. " '*Be through my lips to unawakened earth the trumpet of a prophecy,*' " he exulted. "Jonathan, I'll find you!"

He stood there for a moment, gripped in the illusion of power. Then it receded. Reality pushed at him. Had the boy escaped, somehow, as Ben had said? No, he would have known.

Just for the hell of it he went over to the door he'd forced open to see if there were any way he could lock it from the hall side. To his pleasure there was an old-fashioned sliding bolt high above the original lock. Lawrence moved it across. "That'll keep the little bastard in," he said aloud. When the suspicion that it would be unlikely for Jonathan still to be in the bedroom crossed his consciousness, he pushed it away. The boy was there—somewhere. And he would find him.

Cheryl's body lay in the morgue while the police tried to find out who she was. With all identification removed, she was simply one of the thousands of young women who came annually to the Big Apple with dreams of glory and wealth and love and fame and took the wrong step or met the wrong man. The police knew what kind of gun had killed her, and the coroner's office told them that apart from being shot to death, she was a woman in her early twenties in excellent health. After that they waited for someone to show up who was missing a daughter or a sister or a girlfriend or a wife.

After Mooney and Patrick confirmed that either Barry had given them false information about where Cheryl lived and worked or he had passed on the false information given to him, Mooney dialed Fremantle literary agency and asked for Barry. When he came to the phone, Mooney said, "Either you lied to us about your girlfriend's place of employment or she lied to you. There's no employment agency at that number on West Forty-ninth Street."

"Oh."

"Have you talked to her since we were at your office?"

"No. I called her service and left my name a couple of times, but I haven't heard."

"What's the number of the service again?"

"555-4356."

"Okay. I'll be back in touch."

Mooney put the receiver down, then yelled, "Joe!"

Another detective came to the door.

"What's the word on the service this Cheryl Mason used? I called in the number."

"Seems kosher. Patronized a lot by actors and dancers. Nothing unusual."

"Okay." Mooney picked up the receiver and dialed again.

Somebody answered on the third ring. "Service," a male voice said.

"This is the New York police, Sergeant Mooney. I'm trying to locate Cheryl Mason. Can you give me her address?"

"Just a minute."

There was a silence, then a female voice came on. "Why do you want Cheryl's address?"

"Because we'd like to question her about something."

"We'll be happy to take the message and relay it to her when she calls in."

"When was the last time she called in?"

"Before I answer that question I want to make sure you are who you say you are. What precinct are you with? I'll call you back."

Mooney told her and hung up. After a few seconds his phone rang.

"Well," the woman said, "you seem to be who you say you are. In answer to your question, Cheryl hasn't phoned in for her calls since yesterday morning."

"Can you give me an address for her?"

The woman sighed. "It's a box number. We send her bills there. She pays by check, but there's no address on her checks."

"Which bank?"

"The National. The one on West Forty-second Street."

"All right. Now I'd like to have a list of the calls that have come in for her."

"Okay, but you're going to have to come in in person, with all your credentials. We tell our clients that we give out information about them to no one, and we'd go out of business if we didn't seem to keep our word."

Mooney grunted. It would probably be a waste of time, but he'd have to do it. "If she calls in, let me know. And let me know without telling her that I'm interested."

"Okay."

Later that afternoon he went over and picked up her list of calls waiting. Two of the calls were immediately recognizable as Barry's. Mooney went back to the office and called the two others. One was a bar, and the other turned out to be a pay phone on the street.

"Great," Mooney said to himself. "We're really moving."

Megan disliked calling Martha because she did not enjoy talking with someone who seemed to be half or wholly drunk most of the time. But she was a conscientious woman and felt that the mistake she'd made in misleading Jonathan about the doughnut shop on Court Street might have had consequences and should be reported. So she telephoned.

Martha, who had cleaned up the debris from the shattered bottle and opened the windows to let some of the October air in to dissipate the liquor fumes, was walking back and forth across the living room carpet. In an effort to try to stop her shaking, she had drunk several cups of soup, had eaten some crackers, and had drunk some milk before everything she'd taken in had been vomited up violently and suddenly. Fortunately, there was a bathroom off the living room and she had managed to get there before her stomach projected up the whole mess. A lot of it had gone onto the bathroom floor, but at least it was tile and was easily cleaned. She now felt better, but weak, and decided to take in nothing but water. It was at that point that the phone rang.

"Martha, this is Megan Stanley. There's something I feel I must tell you." And she explained her error in saying to Jonathan that the doughnut place on Court Street was closed. "I suspect he might have gone then to the one on Atlantic Avenue. As I told you this morning, he said he was supposed to meet a friend of his father's, somebody he described as a nice man, there. I gather from Marguerite that he was actually supposed to meet his father. And his father would have gone to the place on Court Street, while Jonathan, because of what I told him, may have gone to the one on Atlantic Avenue."

It was all Martha could do to hold on to her screaming

nerves and not yell at this meddlesome woman whose misinformation might very well have caused Jonathan's disappearance or, at least, caused him to be in a place where he might have encountered danger.

"I'm sorry," Megan finished stiffly.

"I am, too," Martha said. "I wish—" I wish the hell you'd minded your own business, her mind silently shrieked. She said, "Thanks for calling." And hung up the phone.

She dialed Mooney's number but was told he was out of his office. "Please have him call me," Martha said.

"Can I tell him anything?" the man on the other end of the phone said.

"No." And then, "Is Mrs. Leonard there now?"

"Mrs. Leonard? Oh, the lady with the drawing. No, she left a few minutes ago."

"Do you have the drawing?"

"Yes. Do you have any information about it?"

"No—not about that exactly, but about something else. That's what I want to talk to Sergeant Mooney about."

"You can tell me."

But Martha didn't trust the run of policemen in a precinct. This was important and needed Mooney's attention. She didn't want it ignored and then forgotten. "No, please tell him to call me."

Just as she hung up, the phone rang again. She picked it up.

"This is David Jennings," a male voice said.

Martha wracked her brain for a moment before inspiration struck. "Sarah's brother?"

"The same. Sarah told me you were having a hard time, what with this crisis concerning your son and at the same time trying to fight drinking."

"I don't see what concern it was of Sarah's to go around telling various people."

"She's trying to be helpful, because she knows my own long fight with alcohol."

"If you're telling me I should go into the hospital or a

rehab I'll tell you right now I'm not going anywhere until Jonathan is found. When that happens, well, maybe."

"I'm not going to tell you that. I know you want to stay on hand and so would I. I just thought I'd pass on one or two ideas to help you over the hump. Do you have any herb teas?"

"I just drank two cups of consommé, ate some toast, and then some milk, and I've just finished being very, very sick."

"Milk wasn't such a good idea. Try an herb tea, if you have one, and some dry toast. If you have soda, like Coke or Pepsi, that would be a good idea. They have sugar and you need sugar right now. Honey's good. You could put it into the tea. You'll feel better. If you need any more thoughts my number is 555-8956. Hope you feel better." And he hung up.

"Lousy moralist," Martha said. She started walking back and forth again. Then she went to the phone and dialed the number Patrick had given her. The answering tape clicked into function on the third ring. The trouble was, there was no beep and the tape went off. It was impossible to leave a message.

"Goddammit!" Martha yelled, and started walking again. She didn't know how long she'd been doing that when she found herself in front of the storage cupboard in her kitchen. The first thing she saw after she opened the cupboard door was a box of peppermint tea bags. On a shelf above was some honey. She put the kettle on to boil again and rummaged on another shelf. The box of melba toast was there and still unopened.

Five minutes later she was sitting on the sofa sipping some peppermint tea heavily laced with honey and nibbling on some melba toast. After eating two pieces of the latter and finishing the cup, she waited to see if her stomach rose again. But everything rested peaceably.

She continued to sit there, feeling a little less physically uncomfortable than she had since early morning. Across the room the liquor bottles seemed to sparkle and blink in the sunlight. She wrenched her mind away from them and thought instead about Jonathan and everything that had happened. The thing to do, she thought, was to arrange what she knew or had learned in some kind of order:

Jonathan had got up that morning and at seven-thirty had gone to see Megan Stanley's kittens.

He had told Megan that he was going to the doughnut shop to meet a friend of his father's, a ''nice man.'' Horror at the implications of all that washed over Martha. But she forced herself on.

His father, unknown to her, had arranged to meet Jonathan in the doughnut shop on Court Street at eight o'clock. He waited there nearly two hours before he looked in the doughnut shops on Montague and then called the school.

Megan Stanley had told Jonathan that the Court Street doughnut placed was closed. It wasn't, because Patrick waited there. But Jonathan may have gone to the doughnut shop on Atlantic Avenue.

Patrick had hired Barry, an office boy at his agent's, to photograph Jonathan.

Sarah Jennings had notified the police and Sergeant Mooney, and Patrick had left the school and gone to find out if the office boy had shown his pictures to anybody. After that they went somewhere else to find something else.

Katie Leonard had called to say that a man had been loitering around the street near their houses and she had drawn a sketch of the man. She had gone to the precinct to show the sketch to the police to see if they recognized it. . . .

Martha paused as something flashed across her memory and was gone. She put her hands over her eyes and tried to get it back. It wouldn't come, but it had something to do with Katie's sketch.

She stood up, poised to snatch her raincoat and go to the precinct before she remembered that she couldn't leave the phone. Stymied, she stood there, then picked up the phone and dialed Katie's number. There was no answer.

* * *

As time passed and Jonathan heard nothing from below, he took the opportunity to look around. He was in a sort of low, very small attic or storage place. As his eyes got used to the dimness, he realized that there must be some sort of light getting in from outside, because it was not completely dark, or at least it hadn't been. It was not much darker than when he had first scrambled up there.

Moving as little as he could so as not to make any noise audible downstairs, he turned his head and examined all he could see from his posture of lying on his stomach on top of the small trapdoor through which he had come. There were boxes around and a large trunk, and behind the trunk there seemed to be a faintly different light from the rest of the room. Staring straight at it, he decided that behind the trunk there must be a window of some kind. He would have given almost anything to scramble to his feet and examine the room properly, but any sound at all might lead the man below to his hiding place.

Slowly, wriggling and sliding himself forward, he moved towards the trunk and the dim light behind it. When he got there, he peered around the trunk and saw that there was indeed a window, or rather half a window, the other half of which was on the opposite side of the separation wall of the storage space.

Jonathan hesitated to slide around the trunk to the window, because that would mean he'd leave his post and if the man below discovered the square in the closet ceiling, Jonathan would not be near enough to prevent him from opening it up by lying across it. But he decided to risk it. He paused and listened. There was no sound from below. Jonathan pulled his sneakered feet under him in a crouch and silently crept around the trunk to the window.

Outside, the sky was dusk, though not as dark as the interior of the little room, and there were stars and a moon lighting up the roofs below.

Jonathan's heart leapt up. That was the outside world, and seeing it from the window seemed to make it easily at hand.

But he looked down and knew that was a delusion. He was many floors above the street. Far below in the darkness was what looked like an alley. Even if he could open the window he would die if he jumped.

The enclosure of the window was about three inches deep, so the window itself was that far from the end of the wooden wall or divider. Standing, Jonathan tried to slide his narrow body around the rim of the divider. But, thin as he was, there wasn't enough room.

What about shouting?

He could shout, and perhaps someone in another building would hear him. It was certain that the man below would, and would recapture him before people in other buildings or on the street would know what was happening or what apartment to come to.

It was the following afternoon that Barry, having left his fifth message with Cheryl's service, called Mooney.

"I know something's happened to her. She's never left it this long before calling back."

Mooney was beginning to think that, too, but he felt impelled to say, "Maybe she heard that you told me about her involvement with kiddie porn and is lying low."

There was a funny sound on the other end of the phone. Then, "Maybe there's an explanation that we haven't thought of. I mean, perhaps she didn't know what her boss wanted."

"She lied to you, didn't she? She gave you a fake work address. Somebody stole your pictures, and you said she was the only one who knew where you kept the spare key."

"Maybe one of my roommates . . ."

"Do you really believe that?"

Barry didn't. But he remained silent for a moment.

"Anyway," Mooney said, "we checked them out. It's not impossible one of them stole the pictures. But at this stage of the investigations, it doesn't seem likely."

"Couldn't you find out if anything's happened to any girl that's like Cheryl?"

Mooney had been on the point of doing that anyway. "All right."

He called the morgue and asked if a girl fitting the description that Barry had given him had been brought in.

"As a matter of fact," the coroner said, "yes."

"What'd she die of?"

"A bullet through the head. Otherwise she was in good shape, in every sense of the word. Pretty little thing."

"I'm coming down," Mooney said. "And I'm bringing somebody who can give you a definite answer if it's the person I'm interested in." Then he dialed Barry's number again.

Half an hour later he met Barry at the city morgue on First Avenue at Thirtieth Street. Seeing Barry's face he said, "You all right, kid?"

"Yes." Barry suddenly realized his teeth were beginning to chatter and clamped them together.

It was a horrifying experience. He took one look at the damaged face that was uncovered for him and gave something that sounded like a sob.

"That Cheryl?" Mooney asked gently.

Barry nodded, and then burst out, "Yes."

An hour later he was sitting in Mooney's office. Barry had a coffee cup in front of him and was staring at it miserably.

"Okay," Mooney said. "I want you to tell me everything you know about her. Don't leave anything out. Where you first met her, where you've met since, what food she prefers, where she likes to go, what she said of herself."

"Why?" Barry asked. "She's dead. What's the use of picking on her now?"

"I'm not picking on her," Mooney explained. "I'm looking for a kid who's disappeared. Remember? She wanted his pictures and it looks like she had connections with kiddie-porn rings. Do you know what they do to kids? Want me to tell you some details we've learned in trying to catch them and put them in jail? You want that to happen to Tierney's kid?"

"No," Barry cried, almost in tears. "It's just that—that, well, it's so hard to think of her doing that."

"Yeah, I know. But don't bother with that. You've seen Jonathan Tierney. Keep your mind on what might happen to him, and incidentally what might happen to you if anybody here got hold of the idea that you were sort of helping Cheryl along in her porn career."

"That's not true!" Barry blazed out, with more energy than he'd shown all day.

"I don't think it is either. But we need your cooperation." The threat was decently veiled, but it was there.

"So," Mooney went on, "speak!" He switched on a tape recorder. "You don't mind this, do you?"

Barry shook his head.

It was a long, rambling narrative that seemed to go on forever, except when Barry would remember something and then stop, near tears. Mooney stopped him once when the tape had run out and told Barry to wait until he had turned it over. Finally, after forty-five minutes of talk, Barry ran down. They sat there in silence.

Mooney said, "Where's that bar, the Shamrock, you mentioned?"

"On Seventh Avenue near Thirty-sixth Street."

"You didn't actually say so but I had an idea you didn't much like it."

"No. I didn't."

"Why?"

Barry's dislike was built on half a dozen impressions, none of which he really wanted to examine because he didn't want to ask himself why Cheryl invariably chose it when she had a chance. "I don't know," he said now.

"Come on, Barry. You're a bright boy. You have a good eye. You're a photographer. What was it you didn't like there?"

"It was kind of dirty and crummy, I guess."

"So is the Golden Nut, which you go to a lot, and O'Banion's. You've even gone there without Cheryl, and they're not exactly Upper East Side eateries."

Barry didn't say anything, trying to pin down impressions he hadn't wanted to receive in the first place. Mooney stared at him. "So what was it you didn't like about the Shamrock?"

Finally Barry blurted out, "There were a lot of gays there. They'd eye me and I felt uncomfortable, like I should be gay, too, only I wasn't."

"You ever speak to one of them?"

Barry shook his head.

"Did you see Cheryl speak to them?"

This hit the nerve Barry had been tiptoeing around. For a minute he didn't say anything.

"I take it your silence means she did."

"She'd be talking to some of them when I came in." He paused, then went on, sounding acutely unhappy, "Like she'd been there for a while. Maybe gone specially to see them."

"Did you ever talk to her about this? Get mad or something?"

Barry had. His jealousy was always near the surface. "Yeah. She said they didn't mean anything to her. That they were just part of her business."

"She was truthful about that, I guess. But what business did you think she was talking about?"

"I thought they were clients of her employment office." Realizing how green and square he must have looked, Barry blushed red. "I guess I sound like the world's prize moron."

"There's nothing stupid in trusting people. The bad part is that in a city like New York, half the time—more than half—you get into trouble doing it. Where'd you come from, Barry?"

With shame Barry confessed to the name of his small hometown.

"I don't know why you act like it was the family skeleton. I've been up there. It's near a lake, isn't it? One of the Finger Lakes?"

"Yeah." Suddenly the freshness, the clean air, the rather dull but friendly people seemed less awful to Barry. He had worked so hard for his sophistication. For the first time he wondered if it were all to the good.

"I went there once," Mooney said. "On my honeymoon. Stayed in a motel and went boating and fishing on the lake."

"Are you married now?" Barry asked.

"Divorced. Like practically everybody else. Okay, Barry. I'll let you go, but stay in touch if you remember anything you've forgotten to tell me."

Barry got up. He stood there for a minute. "You think the men in the bar there were some of Cheryl's customers?"

Mooney cast a sharp glance at Barry. "You mean like she was a hooker?"

"Of course not. I mean, well, like she was selling pictures to them?"

"Or giving them addresses where they could get more or get a different but related type of service."

Barry shuddered, then said, "G'bye," and walked out.

When he'd gone, Officer Johnson brought over the sketch Katie Leonard had left.

"What's that?" Mooney asked.

"This woman, Katie Leonard, a friend of Mrs. Tierney's, brought it in. Mrs. T told her to. She—the Leonard woman—says this is a picture of a man who was hanging out the street near their houses. Apparently Mrs. Leonard and Mrs. Tierney live close together."

"Did you show her pictures?"

"Yeah. And Mrs. Tierney wants you to call her."

Patrick had spent a sleepless night beside the phone in his sublet. The light on the answering machine was not blinking, which the instructions said would happen when he had a message, so he assumed no one had called. It didn't occur to him that he might have failed to reconnect the tapes properly so that anyone trying to leave a message would just get a click.

He couldn't sleep, so he walked back and forth, fighting the temptation to call Martha or Mooney or the precinct to check up on the latest development. He knew that the news of Jonathan's disappearance would shortly hit the papers because he would by then have become officially missing. And while in some sense that might mean that more resources would be available in the numbers of police involved, Patrick also had a strong feeling that because of his own best-seller status the chances of Jonathan's being quietly returned would be severely diminished. An analytical, intellectual man, Patrick liked to back up his feelings with documented facts, and he couldn't on this. There were equal arguments that the kidnapper of a child of a well-known parent would, out of fright, kill the child.

Even to think such thoughts was so terrifying that he felt he had to move, go somewhere, commit himself to some action. But if by any chance someone called, someone who was holding Jonathan, or Jonathan himself, then he'd want to be here. It was a bind as rigid as a straitjacket.

The next day Martha again sat staring at the array of bottles on the counter between the kitchen and the living room. She had spent the day drinking peppermint tea with honey and nibbling melba toast and waiting for the phone to ring.

It had been a night of horror. She had lain in bed twisting back and forth, her legs thrashing with nervous tension. Every now and then she had dozed off, but she had finally discovered that when she was not sleeping she was better off up, drinking some of the sickeningly sweet tea and watching television. Reading, so much the escape hatch of her earlier life, the comforter and panacea as well as the informer and inspirer, was no good now. She had stared at the page, the words bouncing off her mind like tennis balls off a wall. They meant nothing. Television, however stupid, was better. In fact, the stupider the better. When her searching dial hit a serious documentary or news program she now knew to pass on to some oldie, a crime or detective show. Only that held her interest for even a few minutes.

With yet more tea inside her and another show finished, she'd go back to bed and doze off, only to awake a short time later and go through the same procedure again.

The bottles had danced before her eyes all through the night during her visits to the living room and the television set. But, holding the image of Jonathan in front of her like a standard, she had managed not to go near them.

Now, in the low point of the afternoon, she found she couldn't drag her eyes away.

Oh God, she thought. And then, as though chanting a spell or a charm, she said aloud, "Jonathan. I must stay sober for Jonathan." She forced her eyes away from the bottles. On the floor, near them, lay Susan.

"Where is he, Susan? Where is he?" The pale Siamese, lying on the floor, nose on paws, seemed both relaxed and alert. Martha had never been an ailurophobe, shrinking from cats in some primitive reaction. On the other hand, Susan had never for her been a creature in her own right. She was a toy of Jonathan's who, in Martha's opinion, had received more of his attention and affection than she deserved.

Now Martha got up and went over to Susan and knelt, reaching out her hand to stroke her, to make some kind of contact. But Susan sprang away from her and fled, pigeon-toed, down the hall.

"Goddammit!" Martha yelled. She burst into tears. The phone rang.

"Yes?" she cried into the receiver. "Who is it?"

"David Jennings." Then, "what's the matter?"

"What's the matter? You really want to know? My son has disappeared, I can't leave the house because he might call or somebody who knows where he is might call, his cat won't even let me come near her, as though I had some awful plague, and I haven't had a drink." She was ashamed of the sobbing that shook her. "I'm sorry," she wept. "I'm sorry."

"I'll be over," he said, and hung up before she could answer.

She sat there, half angry, half pleased. I suppose he's going to preach at me, she grumbled to herself. But she couldn't help feeling that the terrible emptiness of the house would, at least for a while, be alleviated.

He was there in less than ten minutes, ringing the bell. She went to the door and found she'd forgotten what he looked like, or perhaps it was that he looked different. From the few times she had met him either at one of the school affairs when he had been a teacher or at some function they both attended, she remembered him as heavy and red-faced. Now, although tall, he looked lean and the flush had gone from his skin.

"Can I come in?"

"Don't lecture me, David," she said. "I'm in no mood for it. But your suggestion about the tea, honey and toast was good. Thanks."

She led the way back into the living room. "Didn't you once teach in the school?" she asked.

"Yes, that was one of my various jobs, which I lost along with the other jobs."

"Until you stopped drinking."

"Until I stopped drinking," he agreed. He had on a gray suit and dark red tie and there was now gray in the dark hair.

At least his gray eyes were no longer bloodshot, she thought. "Well, what good advice do you have for me this time?"

"I take it you haven't heard from or about Jonathan."

"No."

His eyes traveled over the room and stopped. Following his gaze, Martha turned and saw the bottles arrayed in regimental order.

"You know," David said, "I take off my hat to you. If I hadn't had a drink for only one day I could no more bear to have those bottles there than to have a glass full of whisky at my elbow every time I moved."

"Are you suggesting I should throw them out?" It was an

idea that had occurred to her and that she had instantly rejected.

"I would."

"What a waste!"

He looked at her for a moment. "Is there anything I can do? Right now I'm working in a bookstore on Montague, so I'm less than five minutes away. You probably have female friends to do this for you, but if you need to have an errand done and there's nobody else to do it, I'd be glad to help. I'll leave my number here." He scribbled on a piece of paper and put it on the counter under one corner of the phone.

"All right. Thanks."

"I'd better get back. Nice to see you."

He was gone before she fully took in that he was leaving. Martha felt a little let down. She'd expected him to preach at her and she was looking forward to the resentment she'd feel when he did. She could resent his suggestion about the bottles, of course. She was thinking about that when the phone rang.

"Yes?" She knew her reply must sound as frantic as she felt.

"Mooney," the sergeant said. "You left a message for me to call you. Anything happen?"

Martha told him about the pencil sketch that Katie Leonard had left at the precinct.

"Yeah, I saw it. Did you remember who it was?"

"No, not exactly. But I had this—this sort of flash of memory. I've seen that face before. But when I try to pin it down I can't. It goes away. But that's not what I called about. Megan Stanley, a neighbor, called me this morning and told me that when Jonathan was with her yesterday morning he told her he was going to meet one of his father's friends, the nice man he talked about."

"Yeah, I know that. I was at the school. What about it?"

"She remembers now that she told Jonathan that the doughnut place on Court Street was closed for renovations, so he must have gone to the place on Atlantic Avenue. And

I wondered if anybody in that place would recognize that drawing as somebody who'd been there with Jonathan.''

''Thanks,'' Mooney said. ''We'll give it a shot. You're going to be there for the next hour or two?''

''Sergeant, I'm going to be here until I hear something from or about Jonathan.''

8

Leonard's sketch made, Mooney left the precinct with an
envelope containing six. He went first to the doughnut shop
on Atlantic Avenue.

It was larger and more brilliantly lit than the one on Court
Street. Plain wooden tables were spread around the square
area, there were stacks of doughnuts and other pastries under
the counter, and disposal bins dotted the corners and the exit.

"What'll it be?" the young man behind the counter said
as Mooney walked up.

Mooney took out his shield, showed it to the man and put
it back in his pocket. "Sergeant Mooney," he said. Then he
opened the envelope and pulled out a photocopy of the drawing. "Ever see this guy before?"

The man glanced at it and shook his head. "No."

"Please look again."

"I ain't seen him, I'm tellinya."

"Were you here yesterday morning around eight to nine?"

"No. Yesterday was my day off."

"Who was here then?"

"Well, Willie was supposed to be, but he was sick. I guess it was the boss."

"Is he here now?"

"Yeah." He raised his voice. "Nick! Somebody here to see you."

A tall, heavy man came out. He looked to be in his forties and had a harsh, intelligent face. "Yeah?"

Mooney showed the drawing. "Was this man in here yesterday around eight to nine in the morning?"

"Who wants to know?"

Mooney again took out his shield and introduced himself. "Did you see this man or one who looked like him?"

Nick wiped his hands on a paper towel, then took the paper. He stared at it for a moment, then said, "Could be."

"Was he with a boy? This boy?" This time Mooney drew out a copy of the picture Patrick carried with him.

Nick took it in his other hand. "Yeah. I remember this kid. Good-looking. He comes here sometimes, along with the other kids."

"But yesterday he was with this man?"

Nick raised his head and stared out the window. Mooney was almost tempted to turn around to see if he were watching something, but he knew the man was trying to recall the previous day.

"The kid was here first," Nick said. "He came in and sat down at a table. Looked like he was waiting for somebody. Then the man came in. They talked. Then they left. They didn't buy anything."

Mooney felt his heart beginning to thud as it always did when a case had a break. "Ever see the man before?"

"No. What's this about?"

Mooney debated with himself. He preferred to give as little information as possible. But the news would soon leak out. There wasn't any way they could keep it under wraps— not with a well-known writer for a father.

"This kid hasn't been seen since yesterday morning. He

thought he was coming here to meet his father. But this guy is not his father and neighbors have reported seeing him around the house in the past few days. In fact, one of the neighbors drew this.''

''That's too bad.'' Nick looked at the drawing again. ''It's not exactly like him, you know. It's just that you think of him when you see it.''

''Could you give me any other details? Height, hair coloring, eyes, weight, age?''

Nick shrugged and looked back at the drawing. ''About my height, that is, about five eleven. Dark hair, gray around the sideburns, thin, kind of . . . '' He struggled with some thought.

''Kind of?'' Mooney said helpfully.

The man shook his head.

Mooney had an inspiration. ''If you saw this guy, without knowing anything about him, and were just guessing what he did, what would you say?''

Nick said promptly, ''Schoolteacher.''

That was the last thing Mooney was expecting, but he filed it away. ''Okay. I'm going to leave a copy of this with you. Show it to anybody you think might be helpful. If you have any inspiration, call me here.'' Mooney handed him a card. ''And thanks.''

Jonathan woke up with a pressing need to go to the bathroom. He had been conscious of it before he slept. Now it was urgent. He looked quickly around. Light was coming from behind the trunk. He got to his feet. The only things in this small space were the trunk, three or four packing cases one on top of another, and a big pile of newspapers. It would have to be the newspapers, he decided, and crawling over there, relieved himself. When the urine started to flow off the top, he hastily moved some papers from farther down the pile and placed them around on the floor. He was afraid that if the liquid poured over the floor it might leak through into the closet and betray his presence.

In pushing the pile of papers around he made more noise than he had intended, and he waited, holding his breath. There was no sound from below. He then became aware of something that had only sporadically presented itself the night before—hunger. When excited or frightened he had always lost his appetite, so the fact that he hadn't eaten since the morning before only bothered him from time to time. Now it was a raging demand, and far worse was thirst.

Crouched over the trapdoor, he listened. Then, as quietly as he could, he lay down so that his ear was over the crack in the floor where the trapdoor fit. There was no sound that he could hear. Slowly, slowly, he slid his fingers under the handle in the middle of the door, making it look like a lid to one of his mother's coffeepots.

Suddenly, thinking of that, he thought about Martha and then about Patrick. His longing was so great he didn't think he could move. For the first time since he had gone with Lawrence, he felt the tears forcing themselves out of his eyes. Putting his hands over his face, he muffled the sobs he couldn't stop. After a while the stifled sobs slowed, and he wiped the tears from his face.

Once again he slid his fingers under the handle and exerted a little pressure upward. The trapdoor came up easily and without a sound. Jonathan found himself staring down into the near black of an almost completely closed closet. But with a lift of the heart he saw that it was exactly the way he had left it in his frantic climb up and last desperate effort to pull the door to behind him.

It was a risk, but a risk he had to take, so he leaned out of the hole, supporting himself on one hand on the top of a box on the highest closet shelf, and pushed the closet door farther open.

With the door open and by leaning down from his hole he could see a large part of the room and saw that it was empty.

Slowly, careful not to make a sound, he climbed down the shelves, making sure that he pushed nothing that would drop or create a noise by sliding. Finally he was down.

Peering around the door, he saw that the room was indeed empty. Luckily, the carpet was thick so he could cross the floor to the bathroom without making any noise. Once there he closed the door, went over to the basin and filled a glass with water. He drank that and then another glass and half of a third. His thirst appeased, he turned off the water and stood there, listening for any sound. But there wasn't any. Then he noticed that there was a small window at the end of the room. Walking silently over, he looked outside, but there was no fire escape near, nothing but a long drop to the small garden below.

Leaving the bathroom, he went back into the bedroom and crept to the door leading to the hall. Gently he took hold of the doorknob. Gently he turned it. But when he pulled, the door didn't move. He tried again. It still didn't move. There was, of course, the bolt. He stood, afraid, before making any effort to turn it, sure that it would create far more noise flipping over suddenly and noisily. Finally he grasped the bolt and tried to turn it. It wouldn't move. He then took both hands and tried. Nothing happened. He tried again, one hand on the doorknob and one on the bolt, but the bolt wouldn't budge and the door remained firmly closed.

He stood there. The disappointment was so great he could hardly move. How could he get out? How could his mother or his father or anyone ever find him? He would be here forever and would die and no one would ever know. Panic seized him, but something, some instinct for survival, kept him from giving in to it. I've got to think of something, he told himself. What would his father do?

He continued to stand there, his hands up against the door, leaning on it. He tried to think of something. But nothing came. His resolve, so strong a few minutes before, vanished. Suddenly he sat down, not caring if anyone heard him or not. But the apartment seemed totally silent, and the silence that was so reassuring before he discovered the door was locked now appeared threatening. What if everyone had deserted the apartment? What if no one would ever come in again?

With the door locked how could he find something to eat? Would he die here and his body just lie in the room?

"No, no," he sobbed. "Please, somebody help me."

But there was no reply, no sound.

Eventually he stopped crying. Again he thought of shouting and yelling. But remaining caution kept him from trying it. So he sat cross-legged on the floor, his back to the door, staring at the room.

After a while he realized he was staring at the little bureau beside the bed. The furniture was white, as was the bed and the bedspread. The bottom drawer was partly open. Jonathan continued staring at the space between the drawer and the frame it was supposed to fit into. It was several minutes later when he realized he was reading the word "biscuits" on the top of a box that was in the open drawer. He got up and went over to the drawer. Inside was a package that read, "English Tea Biscuits." Opening the top he found several layers of cookies in small piles.

Only just remembering not to shout, he started putting them in his mouth, eating one after the other as fast as he could. After about the fourth he slowed down, remembering hearing somewhere in some class that the slower you ate, the longer the food lasted. But he kept on eating.

He had finished half the box when he heard a slight sound coming from the other side of the door.

He moved quickly, closing the drawer as quietly as he could and tucking the half-finished box under his arm. Carefully he brushed away any crumbs that might have fallen on the floor, and then, moving silently in his sneakers, he went back to the closet, climbed up the shelves and into the hole. He pushed the boxes around to hide the hole, then slid the trapdoor down. The last thing he saw as he slipped it into place was the white telephone on the bedside bureau. I should have called Dad, he thought, furious at himself.

Mooney rang the doorbell and waited.

Martha flung the door open. "Have you found out anything?'' Her fear was so great that it hit him in the chest like a thrown weight.

"A little. Not a lot,'' he said, walking into the living room. "The man in the doughnut place on Atlantic Avenue recognized the drawing Mrs. Leonard had made. He said that was the man who was there and who Jonathan walked out with.''

"Why didn't he stop him? Didn't he know there was something fishy about it?''

"How could he? He took it that the man was a friend of the family's.''

"Couldn't he see—'' She stopped because she saw how it sounded. She hadn't even got up yesterday morning when her son left the house. With far more reason to keep a close eye on her child, she hadn't bothered to see him off to school. In shame she put her hands over her face.

Mooney had a fairly clear idea of how she was feeling but couldn't think of anything helpful to say, so he asked, "Can I sit down?''

She took her hands away from her face. "Yes. I'm sorry.''

He pulled a copy of the pencil sketch out of his pocket and unfolded it. "You said this reminded you of something or somebody but you couldn't remember who it is. Look at it again.'' He handed it over.

Martha took the sketch and stared at it once more. She waited for that flash of recognition, but this time it didn't happen. She kept on looking, but the more she looked the less the man's face reminded her of anything. She shook her head. "Nothing,'' she said.

Mooney got up. "Keep it. It's a photocopy. Put it up somewhere you can see it. Maybe the memory will come back.''

He was gone before she realized he was going. The sketch was lying on the coffee table. Martha picked it up and stared. Still nothing. She put it back on top of a small pile of books and took up her restless pacing. Every now and then she picked up the sketch and examined it in detail. She got so she could describe in detail the man's nose, eyes and chin, the way he wore his hair. Yet the whole lacked impact. She could not bring back that overwhelming conviction that she had seen him before.

Before he left to go over to look at the picture, Patrick called Mooney.

"I tried to get in touch with you," Mooney said. "There's a picture here I'd like you to look at."

"So I heard from Martha. Why didn't you leave a message on the tape?"

"Because it's not working. There never is a beep. It stopped before I could say anything."

"Hell and damnation! I thought I'd made sure that this time I got the reprogramming right. I wonder who else has been trying my phone."

"I'd fix it if I were you. If you can't figure it out, I'd call the place where you got it and ask them to walk you through the programming."

"I didn't get it. It went with the sublet. But I'll call the manufacturer. I haven't dealt with this kind before. Look, about the picture. Can't you come here with it, or send somebody with it? I don't like to leave here, especially with the answering machine not working."

"Okay. I'll send somebody. Even if you don't recognize it, see if you get a flash, like he reminds you of somebody."

"And you say Katie Leonard drew this? Wonders'll never cease. She was always one of my wife's drinking companions."

"By the way," Mooney said, "when I showed it to Mrs. Tierney she didn't recognize it, but she said there was a moment when it suddenly reminded her of somebody, but she couldn't remember who."

"Helpful," Patrick said caustically.

"You must be pretty mad at her," Mooney said. "She's going through a lot."

"Yes. I expect she is, but I have a hard time feeling sorry. If she hadn't spent the last eight months boozing round the clock this wouldn't have happened."

Mooney reflected it wasn't his role to counsel patience to Patrick Tierney, or to express sympathy for Martha Tierney. But he said, anyway, "Kids have been abducted from parents who weren't drinking, you know."

"I take your point. But I repeat, if Martha had been minding the store—looking after the boy whose custody she raised hell to get—he might not be . . . lost." He couldn't bring himself to say "abducted."

Mooney, on the other hand, had just about abandoned any other theory, although he was too good a cop to allow himself to leave any possibility unexamined. "An officer will be around with the sketch soon," he said.

Lawrence was in the kind of blind rage that had become more common since he had been dismissed from his job five years previously. Through a combination of good luck, an excellent lawyer and a fumbling district attorney, he had managed to avoid prison, but he did not see the degeneration of his life as any fault of his own. Those responsible were his iron-fisted, puritanical previous employers, the fascist legal system and the family and friends who had deserted him. The anger that, along with the manic spells, had increased in both frequency and power was now gripping him again.

He had been convinced that the boy was still in the apartment, a conviction that was strengthened by his own revulsion towards Ben Nicolaides, who had insisted that Jonathan had escaped, and by his need to believe that he had not been so stupid as to let the boy get away. He had had experience with little boys and he was sure he was right.

But this conviction had weakened during the night. He had banked on the boy's having to relieve his physical wants— hunger and thirst and his need to use the bathroom. With those urges pressing on him, Lawrence argued to himself, surely no eight-year-old boy had the determination to remain locked in whatever bolt-hole he had discovered. Lawrence did not question himself as to where the bolt-hole might be.

Nor did he allow himself to remember the care with which he had searched in that room, any more than he permitted himself to consider that the boy had successfully eluded him and run away. He also didn't let himself remember Ben's sarcasm and mockery when he had insisted that Jonathan had got out and that he, Lawrence, was crazy. Other people had said that to Lawrence and it always produced in Lawrence a searing rage.

But the boy had not appeared anywhere. And when Lawrence, after a fitful night, had slid the bolt back on the door and peered into the bedroom in which he had previously locked Jonathan, there was no indication that the boy was there. Once again he had looked in every conceivable crevice and had pushed aside the clothes in the closet. Nothing.

Finally, leaving the room and refusing to see it as an empty gesture, he bolted the door again from the outside. Then he left the apartment.

Now he walked east, striding quickly, keeping his head down. He had waked up angry and frustrated and hungry and had gone to make himself some breakfast, only to find there was no coffee left in the apartment kitchen, nor any fresh milk. He had had a vague memory of some English tea biscuits that he had bought on another occasion, but a search throughout the kitchen cupboards and drawers produced nothing. One of Ben's rules was: No perishable food, not even bread. As Ben, a lifelong city resident, explained, you never knew what could go bad and smell and/or develop bugs or, worse still, roaches. These had a way of drifting from one apartment to another through the walls and along the pipes, and the last thing he needed was to have some pest-control inspectors banging on the door.

Lawrence crossed West End Avenue and continued on to Broadway. After buying a newspaper at the corner, and because he did not want to be noticed too near the apartment, he got on a bus, rode as far as Seventy-ninth Street, then got off and went into a hamburger joint. Sitting at the counter, he ordered coffee, juice and a bagel with cream cheese and jelly. In the days when he had held an honored position in a highly regarded profession, he had pretended to scorn such food, and had managed to maintain a near-macrobiotic diet, concentrating on vegetables, brown rice, fruits and whole grains, and would periodically expatiate to his students on the subject of the destructive eating habits of the Western world. His wife and son of that long-ago past had gone along with him, though he was aware that Michael, their son, periodically stole out to have a hamburger with the other kids, or a bagel and cream cheese. . . .

The only feeling he had now for the woman who had been his wife was one of contempt. If she had understood him better, if she had not taken away his son, he would not now be forced to find his companions in back studios and grungy little storefronts.

He opened his paper, bought partly out of habit to see if his name had occurred anywhere for any reason—for there was a time when every paper, however respectable, had carried the account of his disgrace—and partly because it was physically the biggest paper obtainable and he could hide in its folds.

When his breakfast came, he put the paper in his lap for a moment, thirstily drinking his juice. Then, arranging his juice and coffee to fit inside the paper, he raised it again, and went on reading behind his makeshift fortress.

But in that moment when the paper was lowered a man walked in the side door and sat down at the counter running at right angles to Lawrence. For a half minute he caught Lawrence's profile, and, when Lawrence turned towards his coffee, his three-quarter face. The man was in plain clothes, but he was a cop, and something about that face hooked onto something in his mind. Where had he seen it before?

The news hit the afternoon papers and the evening television news:

BEST-SELLING WRITER'S SON MISSING was one headline. "FOCUS" AUTHOR'S SON ABDUCTED was another.

"The police have confirmed that Jonathan Tierney, eight-year-old son of Patrick Tierney and his former wife, Martha Tierney, disappeared on his way to school yesterday morning," said one attractive newscaster. "Patrick Tierney, author of the best-selling *Focus*, and his former wife are divorced. Martha Tierney lives in Brooklyn Heights, where their son attended St. Andrew's School, an elite private school on Remsen Street. Patrick Tierney has only recently returned from abroad and is living somewhere in Manhattan. No further details have been released by the school and Mr. and Mrs. Tierney cannot be reached."

But that had not prevented the various branches of the media from trying to reach them.

"Please, please," Martha had said tearfully into the phone, as the fourth paper and third television station had called, "please leave the telephone free. If Jonathan, or the—the people who have him—are trying to reach me, they won't be able to get through. And please, please don't come around here. If anybody—if somebody who was trying to get in touch found the place surrounded by reporters, I don't have to tell you that it could completely ruin any hope I—his father and I—have for getting him back. I was once a reporter myself, so I know what I'm asking."

And the papers had for the most part complied. They had also—at least for the time being—refrained from printing what was common knowledge in the world of journalism: that two years before, Martha had been fired for unreliability due to alcoholism.

Patrick, too, had had his callers, though not as many, owing to the fact that he was living in a sublet and was harder to track down. But one industrious reporter with contacts in the publishing house that put out *Focus* had run him to ground and called.

"Listen," Patrick said, "this phone has to remain open in case my son, or whoever has my son, is trying to get in touch. Any delay could mean Jonathan's life. I'll let you know the moment I have any news that I can share, but don't risk Jonathan's life. Do you have kids of your own?''

''Yes,'' the reporter admitted. ''Okay. But I'm going to hold you to that promise to call me—not just all the press, but me—if you get any news that doesn't involve his safety.''

Stephen Morgan and Marguerite Stanley had left school together and without too much consultation, had headed for the house across from Marguerite's, a gloomy-looking, red brick structure the worse for many years' neglect. They went around the garden to the back door, and Marguerite beat a special rat-a-tat on the door, amounting to a code.

The door opened a small amount and a thin, pointed face framed in gingery gray hair appeared in the narrow opening. ''All right. Come in, both of you,'' Belinda Beauchamps said. ''Tessa is not eating for me. Maybe she'll eat for you.''

The smell in the house was considerable, but as Jonathan had often pointed out, no worse than the smell in some houses that boasted no more than two cats. ''It's not the cats' fault,'' he was fond of saying. ''People should change the litter more often.'' He was meticulous about changing Susan's pan, partly because Susan had a way of using the bathtub if the pan were less than spanking clean and partly because he didn't want to give his mother any excuse for complaining about Susan. To be fair, he occasionally admitted to himself, she had never made the slightest suggestion that he should get rid of her. But he knew that for some reason he didn't understand, Susan irritated her.

Once Marguerite, who sometimes came home with Jonathan, said flatly, ''She's jealous.''

Jonathan was about to deny that as absurd, when it suddenly struck him it might be true. After that, he was careful to show affection to Susan only when they were alone.

As Stephen and Marguerite now penetrated farther into the house, the smell grew. It seemed least in the kitchen, by which they entered, and most in the halls, where pans with litter lined the walls.

"I like to leave the sitting room free," Miss Beauchamps explained airily.

She was bent now over a large tiger-striped cat who sat hunched up on the carpet. "Come on, Tessa, you know you like fish." As Tessa continued to ignore her, she said enticingly, "Look at all the other kitties. They'd love to have this fish, wouldn't you, babies?" And she forked up a piece of the fish and waved it in the air.

Tessa didn't move or turn her head. But the dozen or so of the thirty-odd cats in residence that were poised nearby, ready to leap at the piece of fish, moved slightly nearer.

"You see?" Miss Beauchamps said.

When Tessa went on showing no interest Miss Beauchamps lowered her fork. "I do hope there's nothing wrong with her." Her voice shook a little.

"Maybe she just doesn't feel like eating," Stephen said, trying to be soothing.

"I know you mean to be helpful, Stephen," Miss Beauchamps said reproachfully, "but there's something wrong. I know it."

There was a silence, while all three humans present pondered, each in his and her own way, a variety of circumstances: that Miss Beauchamps lived on Social Security and a meager pension from her days as a clerk-typist at a large and stingy publishing company; that most of what little money she had went on vet's bills, even allowing for the fact that the vet, a kindly animal lover, only charged her half his usual fee when he charged her at all, so therefore she was honor-bound not to take advantage of his kindness; that Tessa was now seventeen and, with the aid of Alexander, a large and fertile tom, now deceased, had once produced at least part of the household at present sitting around and waiting for the fish.

Marguerite thought, She'll die if something happens to Tessa.

Stephen thought, The stink in here is terrible. They'll take all her cats away if anybody ever finds out.

Miss Beauchamps thought, The only thing that will keep me alive if Tessa goes is that the others have to have a home. I have no money. If she's in pain—

There was a knock on the front door.

All three people froze.

Miss Beauchamps's eyes darted around to see if there were anything—such as a light—that would indicate she was in.

After a short silence, there was another knock.

Finally there was the sound of footsteps going down the stoop.

Before anyone could stop him, Stephen ran to the window.

Miss Beauchamps uttered a stifled shriek. "Don't let them see you!"

"I won't!" Stephen whispered back.

The curtains hanging by the window were once—in the days of Miss Beauchamps's parents—expensive and luxurious. Now the brocade was filthy with dust, rot and the remains of various feline sprayings. Miss Beauchamps had tried to wash and wipe off the dirtier areas, but she had been only partly successful. When pulled, chunks of the curtains were inclined to come away in the hand, a fact Stephen discovered when he pushed one aside so he could peek between the curtain and the equally filthy net half-curtain covering the actual window. Outside he saw two uniformed men and a black-and-white police car.

"They're cops," he said.

In the dim light of the room Marguerite saw Miss Beauchamps's face become sallow. "I bet it's not about you or the cats," she said, frightened by the woman's distraught look. She hadn't the faintest idea of whether she believed what she said or not; she simply wanted to offer some reassurance.

"I bet it's about Jonathan," Stephen said from the window.

"What's the matter with Jonathan?" Miss Beauchamps asked sharply. Of the three children, Jonathan was her favorite. He was the one who actually helped out. He brought cans of food every now and then, when his pocket money allowed, often played with the cats, especially Tessa, attempted to comb and brush them, when he could find a comb and brush, and even cleaned out the litter pans. He was, in Miss Beauchamps's eyes, a boy whose price was above rubies.

"He's disappeared," Marguerite said. "Nobody's seen him since yesterday morning. The police have been at school and everything."

"Oh!" Distress filled Miss Beauchamps. "Oh, I hope nothing's happened to him!"

"Yeah," Stephen and Marguerite said together.

All three went back to staring at Tessa.

"I think maybe you ought to call the vet," Stephen said.

Miss Beauchamps looked down at her pet. Slowly tears came out of her eyes and ran down her cheeks. Getting up, she went to the phone, dialed a number and spoke into the receiver.

"Dr. Morse is going to drop by on his way home from the clinic," she said when she'd hung up. "You know," she said a while later to Marguerite and Stephen, "I once had a conversation with God."

"You did?" Marguerite didn't believe in God, largely because her aunt was a passionate churchgoer. But she was willing to have an open mind. "What did He say?"

"He asked me who I wanted to have with me when I die and cross over into the afterlife. I told him all my cats who had crossed over, too. 'No people?' God asked. 'No,' I said, 'just my cats.' Of course," Miss Beauchamps went on, "I'd like to have you two and Jonathan. And Dr. Morse. But nobody else."

When Stephen and Marguerite were ready to go home through the back door, they came out into the hall, and dim though the lighting was, they saw that a piece of paper had been thrust under the front door.

"Hey! Somebody's left you a message," Stephen said.

Miss Beauchamps clasped her hands. "Oh God! An official health notice?"

"No. It's a picture of somebody. They've written on top, 'If you recognize this man would you please call this number?' "

"I'm sure I won't," Miss Beauchamps said.

"Here," Stephen said, coming back down the hall and handing the paper to her.

Marguerite peered over Miss Beauchamps's arm as she took it and looked at the drawing. "I think that was the man who I saw walking down toward Sidney Place once. He was sort of spooky."

"What do you mean?" Miss Beauchamps said.

"I dunno. He just seemed weird."

"Do you think it's got anything to do with Jonathan?" Stephen asked.

"Why should it?" Miss Beauchamps asked sharply.

"Aunt Megan told me that Jonathan went to the doughnut place on Atlantic Avenue to meet somebody."

"Yeah, but Jonathan was going to meet, well, somebody else." Stephen reminded himself that he was not supposed to reveal what he knew.

"Who?" Miss Beauchamps said sharply.

Stephen shrugged.

"Stephen, that's not an answer!"

"You know what they're saying in school," Marguerite said. "I think Steve means Jonathan was supposed to be meeting his father."

"He didn't meet his father," Stephen said. "His father and mother both came to the school. At least, that's what Cynthia Dean says. She saw them when she passed the head's office."

Marguerite was watching Miss Beauchamps's face. "Do you know who it is, Miss Beauchamps?"

"No," the aging, frightened woman said.

When they got out Marguerite said, "I think she knew who it was."

"Then why didn't she say?"

"Because, silly, if the police ever got into her house, she's afraid they'd take away her cats and have them killed. She's said that lots of times"

"Why should they do that?"

"Something about a health risk. You know how it smells. They'd take them to the ASPCA, and if nobody adopted them in a couple of days they'd have to put them to sleep."

9

THE SECOND BREAK CAME WHEN neighbors in the Tribeca area of Manhattan reported an intruder in the apartment next to them. There had been several break-ins recently. The street on the far West Side was often deserted, and it was fright more than good citizenship that provoked the phone call.

"He's there now. I hear him."

"Okay. We'll be there. Don't try anything."

A police car happened to be not far from the street, and they caught Leo red-handed trying to get down the fire escape, a clutch of Cheryl's photographs and negatives in his grasp.

"So what are these?" the cop asked when they were back up in the apartment, taking the pictures from Leo's hand.

"Nothing. Just garbage."

"Then why're you bothering with them?"

Silence. Leo was crafty and violent, but not too quick mentally.

"Whose pad is this?" The cop looked around the small

apartment. There were glossy photographs mounted on the walls, all featuring a dark-haired, thin girl, each time with a different man. The cop went over and took down one framed photograph. "Not bad," he said. "Not bad at all." He turned it over. " 'Cheryl with Sid Rodosky,' " he read. "So what did Cheryl do, or should I guess?" He turned to where Leo, handcuffed, was being held by the other policeman.

Leo shrugged.

The man holding him by the arm shook it. "Answer the man, buddy."

"How should I know?"

The first cop went over, picked up the photographs that had been taken from Leo and looked at them. They obviously were not what he was expecting to see, because he said in a puzzled voice, "Who's the kid?" Then, with rising excitement, "Isn't that the Tierney boy—the one that's missing?"

Leo stared straight ahead.

The cop walked up to him. "Why are they here? What's the dame here—Cheryl—got to do with him? That is, if this is her apartment. And where do you come in?"

Leo didn't answer.

"Where did you find them?"

Leo remained silent.

"Maybe in the drawer there," the officer holding him said, nodding towards an open drawer in the bureau. The drawer was half out. In it were pieces of underwear and various other articles, but there were no more pictures. The other policeman went systematically through the remaining drawers and the drawers of an unpainted chest that, with chintz drawn in two curtains around the top, served as a makeshift dressing table. There was some costume jewelry in one of the drawers and on top of the dressing table, all of which seemed undisturbed. But there was nothing else of interest.

The cop looked again at the pictures. "Half the NYPD is looking for this kid. We'd better phone this in and get him to the precinct."

It didn't take the police long to learn that Cheryl was now

lying in the morgue. A call was put in to Mooney, who had brought the identifier to the morgue and was now working with a special task force assigned to the Tierney case and the pictures were taken to his precinct.

Mooney looked at the photographs. "That's the Tierney boy all right, and these are copies of the pictures Pinkus took for the kid's father."

The burglary immediately took on larger ramifications.

Mooney and the other policemen questioned Leo, who put on his expressionless stare and said nothing until Mooney accused him of killing Cheryl.

"You can't prove nothin'," Leo said.

Mooney was fairly aware that this was true. The gun that had killed Cheryl had never been located, and probably wouldn't be by now.

"Maybe not about Cheryl, but we can sure tie you to the kid that's missing. He's pretty well known, in case you hadn't heard." And Mooney tossed over a couple of the papers that were carrying headlines about Jonathan and his picture. "Kidnapping's a federal charge, Leo. You were caught holding the photographs that Jonathan Tierney's father had made of him. We know the negatives were stolen from the photographer's files. You have them. Like I said, kidnapping is a federal charge."

"I didn't take him out of the state," Leo blurted out.

"But you know where he is because you put him there, or you helped put him there. Kidnapping a child for immoral purposes is one of the most serious crimes there is. You can get the death penalty for it. Now, why don't you tell us where the kid is. Maybe things'll go easier for you."

Leo licked a mouth that had gone suddenly dry. "I ain't had nothin' to do with kidnappin'. That's not my line."

"What is? Child pornography?"

"I don't know nothin'."

"Sure you do. You knew enough to steal these. Why?"

He'd stolen the negatives because Ben Nicolaides had told him to. "We don't want nothin' tyin' this kid to us" had been Ben's words. His eyes had slid to the glossies that Cheryl had brought him. "It's a pity, though. A kid like that could go far. But go to Cheryl's place and get the photos and negatives. You ain't heard from her, have you?"

"Nah. Not lately."

"She doesn't hook for you no more?"

"Nah." But Leo didn't like to leave it like that. It was obvious Ben hadn't heard that Cheryl was dead. But he would, sooner or later, and Leo didn't want Ben thinking he had anything to do with it. "She said she knew where she could make more money for us."

"Doin' what?"

Leo had shrugged. "Didn't say."

"Well, I don't want her makin' money by telling somebody about those photos. So go get them."

"Why?" Mooney persisted now. "Why did you steal these?" When Leo continued to play dumb, Mooney got up. "Okay, you'll find out what a federal charge of kidnapping can amount to. And take those papers back to your cell. That boy's father's famous. He can pay for a lot of pressure. If you don't mind having that on your back, then it's okay with us. Take him back!"

Back at his desk Mooney stared at the photographs. He wanted Leo to be as scared as possible, but he also knew he didn't have time to spend on letting him stew. Jonathan's life depended on how soon they could find him.

Mooney went to the district attorney's office and put his case. "Leo has something to do with this damn kiddie-porn ring. I'd bet he knows where they'd take a boy like that. We can't let him be in their hands one minute longer than we can help. Leo's sleaze and he probably murdered that girl. But she's dead. Maybe Jonathan isn't yet. What can I offer him to get him to talk about the people in the ring and find out—maybe—where Jonathan is?"

Later that day Mooney went back to question Leo, but nothing he hinted at or finally offered moved him. "I don't talk until I walk from here," Leo said. He wasn't educated, but he wasn't stupid, either.

"We can tie you to this kidnapping, and I told you that's a federal case."

"You ain't got no way to tie me. I don't have nothin' to do with those pictures. I ain't seen 'em before and you can't hang that on me."

Mooney had a sudden longing to kill the man himself. He had managed throughout his professional life to remain remarkably distant from the crimes and criminals he dealt with every day. Don't judge! he'd told himself a hundred times. Let the courts do that. But child pornography was something else. Whenever he thought what might be happening now to Jonathan, what kind of creature the boy could be turned into, his stomach rose, as did his primitive desire to kill any and all who had anything to do with it.

"Let him cool his heels," he said now to the sergeant.

But he couldn't put his usual toughness into the statement. Time meant so much.

Miss Beauchamps stared at the drawing, holding the paper under a sixty-watt bulb at the back of the living room. "Five years?" she said to herself in a conversational tone. "Or is it six? We must go to the basement, Tessa," she went on. "But not until after the vet has come."

Ben Nicolaides saw the afternoon papers when he went out to lunch and they gave him a bad fright. The identification of Jonathan as Patrick Tierney's son was the worst possible news. A boy whose parents nobody had ever heard of was one thing. The child of a celebrity was another. Then, no sooner had Ben returned to his grimy office above the film-developing store than he heard from one of his informers and henchmen that Leo had been picked up for breaking and entering. After sitting and thinking for a while, he turned on a radio he kept in his office and moved the needle to an all-news station. It was only five minutes from the hour, so he waited patiently through endless commercials and minor stories to the main news at the hour.

Fifteen minutes later he had learned that the body of a woman who had been in the morgue for a day and a half had been identified as Cheryl Mason, that a small-time hoodlum who had always been associated with prostitution had been caught breaking and entering the apartment of the said Cheryl Mason, and, when caught, was clutching negatives of pictures of Jonathan Tierney, the boy who had disappeared.

After listening a few more minutes to make sure nothing else was going to be relayed, Ben turned off the radio and dialed the number of the apartment on 102nd Street.

"Ya better get out of there," he said. "The kid's big news now, and it turns out his father is some kind of a celebrity. Did ya know that?"

"I know his father is a writer."

"Writers are a dime a dozen. This guy's an author, a celeb. I'm tellin' ya, ya better get out of there. Better still, leave the city."

"I'm not leaving while Jonathan's here."

"Are you crazy? How many times do I have to tell ya? He's split! He's not there."

"If he's escaped, then why hasn't he gone to the nearest precinct—or home? He's not a stupid boy and his people are sophisticated and educated. I know he's in this apartment—or maybe I mean the building—somewhere. I don't know where, but I have an idea of how to find out."

"You wanna go to jail for the rest of your life?"

"I'll be careful." And Lawrence hung up. He was in an exalted mood. A sense of power gripped him. He knew the boy was in the building somewhere. Ben had simply joined all the others to thwart him, as indeed had society as a whole, dating back to the days when his wife turned on him. . . . He closed his eyes while the heady rage filled him like a tonic. He was right. He'd always been right. Then he thought of the boy and a scorching hunger replaced the exaltation. It was a relationship that he had been looking for all his life, even before he knew what it was he wanted: teacher and pupil, Socrates and Plato. The Greeks, the wisest of them all, knew the secret of love. Now he knew and no one, not Ben, not the police or the boy's parents were going to thwart him. He would teach that divine boy about love. . . .

In the meantime, seeing the super in the lobby when he came back from breakfast had given him an idea. Getting up suddenly, he left the apartment and went downstairs, hoping that the super would still be there. But he was no longer in the hall. Lawrence hesitated for a moment, then searched the small lobby and the even smaller vestibule outside the locked front door for a sign or notice saying where the super could be reached. Eventually he found it: SEE BASEMENT.

Lawrence got back in the elevator and punched the letter B. When the doors opened he found himself in a large underground room that contained various devices for repair and maintenance of the building. In the corner was an office. Lawrence walked over there and found the super. He had his story prepared.

"A friend of mine said he had stored his trunk somewhere in the eleventh-floor apartment—11B, that is. I've looked everywhere"—Lawrence gave a mechanical-sounding laugh—"in the closets, under the bed, and I can't find it. Then I remembered his letter told me to ask you—that you knew everything about the apartments and would know if there were attics or holes where he could have put his things." Suddenly and obviously Lawrence was holding a twenty-dollar bill.

The super looked at it and counted the cost of what cooperating with this jerk might mean. He had replaced the original super, who had been induced to retire, and was now paid by Ben in addition to the salary he received from the remote and uninterested owner of the building. Ben paid him partly to find his living quarters outside the building, and partly to turn a blind eye and ear to anything—any disturbance of any kind—emanating from 11B. So far, his healthy salary had required very little. But twenty dollars was twenty dollars, he thought, still looking at the bill. It was important that he stay on the right side of the tenant of 11B, but this man must be a friend of the tenant's, so what would be the harm of earning the twenty dollars?

"It's the top apartment so there's a sort of attic, or crawl space above the ceiling," he said. "Maybe your friend's trunk is there." His hand moved towards the twenty dollars.

Lawrence pulled it back. "How do I get up there?" he asked.

"There's a trapdoor in the closet of the main bedroom. You can't see it very well because it's way in the corner and the ceiling paper was picked so it wouldn't show. But it's there."

"I was right!" Lawrence exulted, handing over the twenty dollars. "I was right!"

Jonathan lay across the attic floor, staring out the attic window, filled with despair. It had been almost two full days since he had come here and he was now desperately afraid that no one would ever find him. He didn't know what to do. He could go down into the bedroom, but he couldn't get out from there. He could also be caught by that terrible man, and Jonathan, a New York City child, had a pretty good idea of what the man would do once he got hold of him. There were other problems. The English tea biscuits had long since gone. He was hungry and thirsty again and he wanted to go to the bathroom.

"Dad," he whispered. "Dad! Where are you? Mom?" His rage at his alcoholic mother continued. The whole thing was somehow her fault. But despite himself, he kept remembering scenes from the good times, when she laughed with him and read him stories and made up things to tell him or recited poetry or funny jingles to him. He had waked up with one of them running in his head: *From ghoulies and ghosties and long-leggety beasties, And things that go bump in the night, Good Lord, deliver us!*

"Have you ever counted up the people the good Lord hasn't delivered?" his cynical father once asked.

"Shush!" his mother had rebuked, jokingly, because those were the good days. And she sent Jonathan off to Sunday school, which, on the whole, he rather liked because it consisted mostly of stories about heroic people like David, and he liked such stories.

Remembering those, he wept, lying on the floor, his head on his hands, because he tried to muffle his sobs. He thought about Susan, and her funny, stiff-legged walk and her nice smell and her crossed blue eyes, and he cried again. He was lying there, thinking of Susan when he heard, distantly, the sound that he now associated with the closing of the apartment front door. He held his breath. The man could be coming in or going out.

Earlier that morning Jonathan had drifted off to sleep and only waked up to hear the sound of the front door being closed. His heart had leaped up then, but this sound was followed by the ringing of the telephone, which was picked up on the second ring. By sliding over and putting his ear to the crack in the trapdoor, he had heard the faint noise of the man's voice talking, and he knew then that the man must have been out and had just come back in. It made him sick to realize that his captor had been out while he was asleep.

But now he heard the door again. After that there was no sound at all, none of the distant noises he associated with the man's being in the other bedroom: water flowing, television voices, talking on the telephone, the toilet flushing.

Quietly, not making a sound, he slid over to the trapdoor and listened with his ear to the crack. There was total silence. Jonathan counted to fifty. Then, gently as he could, he lifted the trapdoor and put it to one side. He stopped and listened some more. After that he climbed down and tore to the bathroom. As soon as he finished there he went to the telephone and dialed the number his father had given him and he had memorized. He heard the phone at the other end ring three times. Then there was a click, and he gathered himself to leave a message, but there was no beep. The machine had just gone off.

Jonathan couldn't believe what had happened. But he knew he didn't have any time to bother about it. He dialed his home, and with a feeling of relief beyond anything he'd ever known he heard his mother's voice. "Hello? Hello?"

"Mom!" Jonathan sobbed into the phone. "It's me."

Within half an hour Sergeant Mooney had received two tentative identifications of the sketch that Katie Leonard had drawn and he had had photocopied and distributed to all the precincts.

The first was from an anonymous woman calling from a public phone.

"You don't know me," the rather high-pitched voice said. "But that sketch of a man the policeman was handing out looks like Lawrence Miller, you know, the college professor who was arrested for child molesting. It was six years ago— a well-known college in New England."

"Who is this?" Mooney demanded, his heart beating.

"I'm not going to give my name and I'm calling from a public phone, so it's no use trying to get it traced. Good-bye." And she hung up.

Miss Beauchamps hurried away from the phone on Court Street. It hadn't taken her long to search through the newspapers she kept in her basement, waiting for her to do the research on contemporary history that she had always planned to do but which had been postponed by the more important need of rescuing stray cats. And she had remembered that case particularly, because when disgrace overtook him the professor was teaching at the college her father had once attended.

She disliked the police, whom she looked upon as part of The Enemy, ready to pounce on her and her beloved strays, but Jonathan was in danger, and for him she had to do her part.

The second call came as Mooney was distributing the information about Lawrence Miller to the various precincts and waiting for information about him and his most recent whereabouts to come up on the computer.

"This is Detective Kowalski. That guy in the sketch you were giving out, I think I've seen him."

"Where?"

"In a hamburger joint on Broadway near Eightieth Street."

"When?"

"Around nine this morning."

Mooney sighed. "I wish you'd called me sooner. It looks like this guy has abducted a kid, an eight-year-old boy, and another caller has just said he was once a college professor who got into trouble molesting a boy about six years ago."

"I'm sorry. Things are kind of hectic."

"You say Broadway near Eightieth. Have you seen him there before?"

"No."

"Did he look like he once could have been a teacher in a college?"

"Yeah. Yeah, he did."

Mooney remembered the man in the doughnut joint on Atlantic Avenue. He thought the guy looked like a schoolteacher, too.

"Thanks," he said, and hung up.

"Darling," Martha said. "Darling, are you all right? Have they, has he—"

"No, but I know he's going to find me, Mom. I'm stuck in a kind of attic. I can't get down when he's in the house."

"Where are you?"

"I don't know."

"Think, darling. How did you go there?"

"We went to the zoo first. Then he took a cab and we came here."

"Where's here?"

"Somewhere in Manhattan. West Side."

"Can you remember the street number?"

"No, he said we were going to meet Dad. I wasn't looking."

"Can you remember anything, darling, anything at all? You're good at remembering things. Do you remember when you recalled a house in the country we were looking for had a red barn beside it? Can you think of anything like that?" Please, God, please, she thought. Help him to remember something.

"The door's black. It's sort of an apartment building. There's a funny knocker on the door, a leopard's mouth with a ball in it. To the left I could see the river. Next door, in the window there was a cat and some yellow flowers like the ones you brought home that Susan knocked over. Do you remember, Mom?"

Suddenly Martha thought of something. "What's the number there, Jonathan? Look on the phone!"

Jonathan looked, but as he did so he heard the click of the apartment door lock. Quickly, as quietly as he could, he put the phone back and ran back to the closet, his sneakered feet flying up the shelves. He lifted himself into the attic and replaced the trapdoor. The whole operation hardly took half a minute. Then he lay on the door, his ear to the crack, listening. He heard the voice of the film man first.

"I want ya out of this place. The boy ain't here. But the cops already have pictures of you. Some of my boys have got the word from the precincts. And I don't want nothin' that's gonna lead them here. There's a car downstairs. I'll take you anywhere you want. But I want you outa here."

"The boy's here, I know. I just asked the super if—"

"You did what, you stupid jerk? Do you want to send the cops an invitation? Why don't you call them up?"

"Don't worry. That dumbo didn't know what I was talking about. I just asked about a trunk that a friend left but I couldn't find. He said there was a sort of half-attic or crawl space with a trapdoor in the closet in that bedroom. That's where the boy's been. I'm going to get him now."

"Are you crazy? There are already cops around the area. I've seen them."

"I'll just get the boy now. Then we can take him with us. I've been planning everything."

"You moron! I had that crawl space sealed up a year ago. I wasn't going to have that there with all the work we do in that room. I tell you, he's not there." It was a lie, but anything was worth getting this maniac out of the house and out of the area. If the police stumbled on this apartment, a great deal of expensive equipment would be lost and they'd probably be able to trace it to him and his associates. "It's sealed," he said finally. "Now, let's go."

"Who's that?" Lawrence said, looking past his shoulder.

It was an old trick but it worked. The man turned and therefore didn't see the heavy bronze figure of a naked man coming crashing down on his bald head.

Martha finally got through to Mooney after four tries. Every line seemed to be busy.

"He called me," she burst out when she finally got him. "Jonathan called me. He's okay as of now."

"Tell me everything he said."

Martha went through it. "He said they went first to the zoo and then into Manhattan on the Upper West Side."

"Did he say where?"

"No. But he said there was a house next door with some yellow flowers and a cat in the window."

"We got a report from a detective who saw Miller at a hamburger joint at Eightieth and Broadway. By the way, we know now it's a guy named Lawrence Miller who was once a professor at a college up in New England."

"I was there for one summer school years ago. He taught English. My God, that's where I remember him from! Then he got in trouble."

"Yeah, there was some question about his molesting a kid. He managed to keep out of jail, but he lost his job and his family. He was hospitalized for a while, but you know how that is. They release them with medicine they're supposed to take. Anyway, he's been a drifter ever since. Tell me, what was he like? What d'you remember about him? I don't know whether this'll help, but anything we know is to the good."

Martha pondered. She was impatient because she was frantic for them to get away and start looking, but as he said, anything might help. "He was attractive, in a strange sort of way. Lots of the girls had crushes on him. He was like—well, one of the girls I knew said he was like a mystic."

"Is that what you thought?"

"Sometimes, I guess. But other times, he seemed . . . unstable. Not quite . . . balanced."

"Anything else?"

"I can't think now."

"Okay. Thanks. Listen, try not to worry. We've narrowed it down. There are police all over the West Side looking. Now I have to go. I'll keep in touch." And he was gone.

Suddenly Martha remembered about the black door and the leopard's-head doorknob. Quickly she dialed Mooney's number again. But it was busy. She kept trying, but when she finally got through he was gone.

"Damn, damn, damn, hell and shit!" she yelled. Then she dialed Patrick's number, but after three rings there was nothing but a click. Frantically she paced back and forth. And once again saw the bottles across the room. She wanted her son more than she had wanted anything in her life, but almost as much she wanted a drink. "I can't drink now," she cried. But it would make her head clearer. She'd stop being so nervous. She could think. . . . She found herself walking over towards them. Then on the slip of paper David Jennings had left on the counter she saw his number.

Lifting the phone she dialed, with no idea what she was going to say. She recognized his voice when he answered. "Bookshop," he said.

"I'm going to look for Jonathan and I want a drink."

"Don't pick it up. Whatever else you do, don't pick it up. It won't make anything better. It'll make it worse."

His voice had a curious soothing effect. "Okay," she said. "Thanks."

"Where are you going to look?"

She told him about the phone call and what Mooney had heard about its being on the Upper West Side.

"I can imagine how you feel, but wouldn't it be better to let the police do the looking? They know more about how to do it."

"But they don't know what Jonathan told me about the black door and the leopard's-head doorknob. I have to go."

"Why don't you call them and tell them?"

Suddenly her being part of the search was overwhelmingly important. "I'm going to go myself and look."

There was the faintest pause. Then, "I'll go with you. Shall I meet you at the subway?"

"I was thinking of taking a cab."

"The subway's faster."

"All right. I'll meet you at the subway."

10

JONATHAN, *LYING FLAT ON THE DOOR*
of the attic, his ear against the crack in the trapdoor, had
heard the murmur of voices from the outer room followed by
a strange muffled sound. Then there was a noise that could
be the bedroom door opening. Lawrence's voice, nearer and
clearer, rang out.

"I'm coming after you, Jonathan. I know where you are.
You won't be sorry."

The voice came closer rapidly. There were noises immediately below the trapdoor. Then Jonathan felt the door lifting below his cheek.

Panic filled him. Frantically he slid till his chest was over
the trapdoor and he tried with all his strength to keep the
door down, but it was rising inexorably.

"There you are, Jonathan!" The voice rang with a note
that made Jonathan's flesh creep. Then, despite all the weight
Jonathan could put on it, the door lifted more and somehow
was pushed to one side. Jonathan saw the man's face, the
dark eyes bright and wide open.

Jonathan lifted the square trapdoor, then brought it, corner down, on the face that was now above the floor level of the little attic.

Lawrence gave an angry cry and ducked back, one hand over his nose. "You little—" A stream of filth came from his mouth. Jonathan picked up one of the boxes on the attic floor and threw it down. By pure luck it landed on Lawrence's face just as he was taking his hand away. For a moment he seemed to float, then he lost his balance and fell back.

"I'll get you!" he yelled.

Jonathan didn't wait. Slamming the door down, he moved to the trunk and shoved it with all his might over the trapdoor. It was heavy, far heavier than he had imagined, but fear lent him strength.

Hands below were trying to raise the door as Jonathan pushed.

A final shove, and the trunk slid over the trapdoor.

Heaving, his face red, Jonathan watched as the trunk seemed to hiccup from time to time as the man below tried to move it off the door. To add all he could, Jonathan sat on the lid of the trunk. He could feel, shuddering through his thighs, the frantic efforts of the man to raise the trapdoor with the trunk on top.

"Please," he whispered, not really knowing whom he addressed. "Please make it hold." Somehow the picture of Alec Guinness in *Star Wars* crossed his mind. "The Force be with me," he said to himself. "Please, please don't let him push it away."

After a while the prods from below stopped. There was a short silence. Then Lawrence's voice rang out. "You haven't anywhere to go, Jonathan. I'll have you yet. And it won't be as pleasant as it could have been—at least not for you. You'll pay for this." The word ended almost in a snarl.

With the trunk over the door Jonathan couldn't hear what was going on below as well as he had. He had no idea whether Lawrence had left the bedroom or left the apartment.

Then, suddenly, when Jonathan had convinced himself that Lawrence had left the apartment, his voice came, clear with rage, right below.

"I can do a lot of things to get you out. I can build a fire below here. Nobody will be able to get to you then. Fire goes up. You'll be dead with the smoke before it reaches you, but if you aren't, then you'll burn to death."

There was a silence. Then in a different voice Lawrence said, "All I want is to give you love, to show you how love is made. You'll like it. Not many boys get this opportunity." Another silence. Then, "What do you want, Jonathan, love or fire?"

Jonathan sat there, his legs shaking, as he smelled the first tinge of smoke coming through the cracks around the trapdoor and from under the trunk.

Having given up trying to find by phone a repair service that would send someone to mend his answering tape right away and frantic because until that was done he remained a prisoner in his apartment, Patrick bolted out onto the street and offered a generous bribe to a local repairman if he would just return with him and fix his tape. Almost dragging him back, Patrick said, "As I've explained, it's an emergency. Now, fix this goddam tape so that people can reach me even if I'm not here." He paused. "That doesn't make sense, but you know what I mean."

The man played with the little tapes and the buttons on the machine. "You've done the whole thing wrong, Mr. Tierney. A smart man like you! I've got kids who can do this."

"Being mechanically deft is not my forte, but it is yours. Please do it as quickly as you can."

Martha and David got out of the West Side subway at Eighty-sixth Street.

"I still think we should have gotten out at Seventy-ninth," David said. "It's a lot nearer to the Eighty-first area where the police say Miller was seen."

"I don't know why I keep thinking that it's north of here. I just do. Why don't we split up?"

David hesitated. As he knew all too well, he would, under similar circumstances when he was drinking, use splitting up as an excuse to make for the nearest bar. But Martha's son was at stake. She was almost rattling to pieces, but she swore she'd not had a drink since she heard of Jonathan's disappearance, and she was in bad enough shape for him to believe it.

"Okay," he said. "You go north and I'll go south. But supposing either one of us finds it?"

Martha hesitated. "What I'd rather you do," she burst out, "is to help me go east and west on the streets. I don't feel he's south of here, and if he could see the river I don't think he'd be east of Broadway. But he could be either side of West End. Anyway, as we finish each street we can check with each other on West End."

"All right."

"Remember, a black door, a leopard's head with a ball in its mouth as a knocker and a yellow flower in the window next door. Also a cat, though the cat's probably moved a thousand times since he saw it."

"And the flower can have been moved, too. Okay, I'll take the streets east of West End, you take the west."

Martha walked rapidly along Eighty-sixth Street on the south side and then broke into a run. It became obvious that the kind of door she was looking for was not among the apartment buildings on Eighty-sixth Street west of West End. Nor were they along the north side. At the end of Eighty-sixth, she rounded the corner at Riverside Drive, ran a block north, then turned into Eighty-seventh Street. As she sped along, she checked the doors on both sides of the street. When she reached West End, she saw David emerging onto the other side of the avenue. He waved and turned north, too. She waved back, ran up West End to Eighty-eighth and turned in there.

On several streets she found there were no black doors and

no knockers that could be described as leopards' heads. There were lions' heads, but Martha was fairly sure that Jonathan, cat lover, would not confuse a leopard with a lion. And furthermore, in each case, the doors were red, green and blue, but not black.

She went on, mostly walking as quickly as she could, occasionally running. But her breathing was not up to the task, and sometimes she had to bend double, holding her side, trying to get sufficient air in her lungs. What was it some doctor had said to her? "Aside from anything else, Mrs. Tierney, there's nothing that can break down the body as fast and as completely as liquor, not at the rate you're drinking." At one time, almost sick with her inability to draw her breath, she was afraid that she would vomit right there on the nice-looking sidewalk between West End and Riverside.

Once David had come over to her, running easily. "Are you all right?"

"Yes," she said, her breath heaving. "Have you found anything at all that sounds the way Jonathan described?"

"No. Wouldn't it be a good idea to call in the descriptions to the police?"

"They're always busy and Mooney wasn't there when I tried to call before. If you're tired" she heaved sarcastically, "you don't have to go on."

"I'll go on," David said somewhat grimly, and just managed to keep himself from pointing out that he was in far better shape at this moment than she.

One of the policemen used his walkie-talkie to get in touch with Mooney. "Didn't she give you any idea about what the door looked like?"

"No," Mooney said shortly. "But I'll check with her."

He telephoned and listened as the phone rang and rang. Finally Martha's voice came on tape, asking him to leave a message. Angry because he thought she should have stayed at home in case Jonathan or anyone tried to reach her, he left a message asking her to call him. Then, because he realized this would send her hope soaring, he added that if Jonathan had given any description of the house where he was being held, he wanted to have it.

As soon as Jonathan smelled the smoke, fear gripped him. For a moment he couldn't move. Then, "No!" he cried. "No! No!" Then he yelled, "I'll come down! I'll come down!" He could somehow fight for himself when he got down. It was a better bet than being burned to death.

Lawrence heard him, but the fire, catching on the tinselly clothes in the closet, was suddenly out of control. His exaltation collapsed. Frightened, he retreated into the bedroom and towards the door. As he hurried out of the room he heard Jonathan scream. "Serves him right," he muttered.

His tape now properly installed, Patrick called Mooney, only to discover he was out. Then he called Martha and got her tape. Not finding Martha sent up his anxiety. Would she leave the house unless she'd heard from Jonathan? His heart started beating. He called Mooney's office back and asked to speak to somebody there.

After he had announced who he was, he asked if there was any further news about his son.

"Sergeant Mooney is up on the Upper West Side now trying to find where the house is."

"What do you mean?" Patrick yelled. "Have you heard from Jonathan?"

"Mrs. Tierney heard. The boy called her. He said he was being held somewhere on the Upper West Side."

"Why the hell didn't she call me?"

"Maybe she did," the officer said. He'd been there when Mooney tried to leave a message. "But when the sergeant tried to leave a message, your answering machine didn't work. Maybe it didn't work if Mrs. Tierney tried."

"Probably," Patrick said bitterly. "Do you know where on the Upper West Side?"

"I'm sorry. That's all I know."

Patrick almost threw down the phone and bolted from the apartment.

Dripping and panting, Martha came to a brief rest on the corner of Ninety-ninth Street and West End Avenue. Unless she'd missed the black door and the leopard's head, there was nothing so far that remotely resembled Jonathan's description, and this was considerably north of Eightieth Street. Had she been wrong to insist that David patrol east of her, rather than south?

She stood, one hand gripping the top of one of the new pay telephones. After a minute she looked down at it. Since for the moment she couldn't move, she might as well check her own phone to see if Mooney had left any more information.

What she got was his angry query about any further descriptions. "But I told him," she said aloud, as David came running up.

"Who're you calling?" he asked.

She answered as she dialed Mooney's number.

"Just a minute," the man who answered the phone said when she identified herself. In a second Mooney picked up the phone. "Mrs. Tierney?"

"Yes. I didn't tell you about the black door and the knocker like a leopard's head, did I?"

"No. Why didn't you tell me this before?" Then, "Never mind. I guess you thought you did. You're at home now, aren't you?"

"No, I'm at the corner of Ninety-ninth and West End."

"I want you to go back home. I'm not sure what we're going to find and I need to have you to refer to."

"I'll call you at the street corners from time to time. He's my son and I'm going to look for him." Then, because she was tired and sweating and so nervous she felt sick, she started to cry.

David looked at the dripping face. It was a mild fall day, but it was far from hot. "Are you okay?" he asked.

"I'm fine," she all but shrieked. "Now, let's keep going!"

Ben came to with the smell of smoke in his nostrils. There was a terrible pain in his head and he felt nauseated. At that moment Lawrence flung open the bedroom door.

"What happened? Where's the fire?"

"It started in the closet," Lawrence said briefly.

Ben's head cleared a little. "You started it."

Lawrence shrugged. "He wouldn't come down." His eyes narrowed. "You lied to me. You told me the attic was sealed. It wasn't. That blasted kid was up there. Well, I showed him. Let him fry!"

Ben rose to his feet and gave a shout of pain. "You're destroying all the tapes. You crazy jerk! What do you think I kept up there? All the tapes!"

He pushed his way into the bedroom, then started back. A stream of obscenities poured out of his mouth. But loud as they were, they didn't cover the sound of the fire engines clanking and shrieking towards them.

Jonathan, half insane with terror, stood still, then tried to remember everything he'd heard in his school fire drills. Get some water to soak towels. There was no water and no towels. He started whimpering with fright, like a small animal, and then he began coughing. Smoke poured from around the edges of the big trunk. Jonathan put his hand on it, with half an idea of pushing it out of the way to enable him to get below, but he snatched away his hand with a cry. The metal trunk was red-hot. Turning desperately, he saw the window, or rather the half of the window on this side of the wooden divide.

If he could only wriggle past the end of the divide! But he had tried that and failed. Then he recalled more advice from the school drills: Get down near the floor. There's less smoke there. He crouched down, but because the smoke was coming up from the trapdoor, it wasn't much help. He took a deep breath and felt the burning down into his chest.

"Please," he whispered. "Please help me!"

He then went towards the window and stood up, pressing his body against the end of the divider. The space was only a few inches wide. He pushed and squeezed and held in his stomach and chest. He couldn't do it. He almost gave up hope then.

He heard the fire engines racing into the street. Turning aside, he kicked his foot through the window, kicking it again and again as he screamed, "Help! Help! Help! Help!"

His leg was bleeding from a shard of glass. But by kicking a hole in the window, he could shove past the divider. He gave a final push and found himself in the front half of the attic. A window there gave out onto the front.

Bleeding, coughing, he ran towards it and, taking up a box, threw it through the small window. The firemen, summoned by anxious neighbors, saw him then, and the huge ladder started pushing up and turning.

It was Mooney who saw the two men erupt through the front door and onto the street and he stopped them cold with his drawn pistol. "Professor Miller," he said, "and our old friend Ben Nicolaides." As the two men were cuffed, he said, "If the firemen don't get to that kid in time, you're going up for murder."

"I tried to get to him," Lawrence screamed.

"Like hell he did. He lit the fire!" Ben, up for God knew how many counts of pornography, wasn't about to take any rap for child murder.

'Okay, son," the fireman said. "Now, take hold of my shoulders with both hands. I'm going to put my arm around you and then slowly turn you around so you come down the ladder. I'll be holding on to you, so don't worry!"

* * *

"Jonathan!" He heard his mother calling as she ran along the street. "Jonny darling! Be careful, be careful!" And then, because it sounded so ridiculous in view of what he had gone through, she started to laugh, and then began crying.

Eventually Jonathan was down. She saw him reach the ground and stand a little unsteady for a moment. He began to run towards her. As she went to meet him he seemed suddenly to have a light shimmering around his head. Then she was thrashing around on the ground, her arms and legs pumping spasmodically.

The gathered crowd murmured.

"Get back," Mooney roared, coming forward.

Jonathan stared. It was the final horror. He started to cry. As he turned away, his father ran to him and held him close, his face turned away from whatever hideous thing was happening to his mother.

David and one of the firemen were holding her so that she wouldn't hurt herself or swallow her tongue. As Mooney came up, David said, "It's a convulsion."

"Is she epileptic?" Mooney asked.

"No, at least I don't think so. This is very common in withdrawal. She hasn't had anything to ease it for the last two days, and she hasn't had anything to drink."

Martha came to to see Mooney and David bending over her and, a few feet away, Jonathan with his face against his father. Patrick, his arms around his son, was also watching her. Beyond him were more police, firemen, and a crowd. She wondered what they were doing there. Then she realized she was lying down, and tried, feebly, to sit up.

"Don't push yourself," David said.

"What happened?" she murmured.

"You had a convulsion," David answered.

"A convulsion?" A memory floated into her mind. "Katie said I could have one if I didn't have a drink." She paused, and then, as more memory flooded in, "Jonathan!"

"He's all right," David said quickly.

"Jonathan!" she cried again and this time managed to sit up. Memory was beginning to come back. "Oh God!"

Jonathan turned his face towards her. All he could think about was the way her body had been thrashing. He clung to his father.

Martha struggled to her feet. "Jonny darling." She tried to move, but a fatigue beyond anything she'd ever known seemed to hold her feet. "Did he hurt you, darling?"

Jonathan shook his head.

An officer walked up and said to Patrick, "There's an ambulance here. We sent for it when—when Mrs. Tierney had the convulsion. Maybe she and Jonathan could go together in it, because we think he ought to be looked at, too, to make sure he's okay."

"Can I go with them?"

"Sure."

The emergency section of the hospital was controlled pandemonium. Patrick and David sat in the waiting area. They had been there for what seemed like an eternity. No one had invited David along, but he had come anyway, and at one point, after murmuring something about talking to the doctors, had got up and pursued a couple of them down the hall. When he returned, Patrick, not too pleased, said pointedly, "I don't think I know you. And what's your interest in all this?"

David held out his hand. "David Jennings. I'm an alcoholic—a recovering alcoholic—myself. Sarah Jennings, the head of St. Andrew's, is my sister. Before I drank myself out of the job, I used to teach at the school and met Martha there. After that I picked up a drink again and finally landed in a rehab. Now I work in a bookstore in the Heights and go to a lot of AA. Sarah called me the other day to see if I could interest Martha in the meetings."

"And you couldn't, I'd bet my bottom dollar," Patrick said grimly.

"She said that as long as Jonathan was missing she wasn't going anywhere. And I can't fault her for that."

"I guess not." Patrick stared down at his hands for a moment. "According to Sergeant Mooney, it was my hiring my agent's mailboy and general gofer to take pictures of Jonathan that started the whole thing."

"How so?"

'He showed them to his girlfriend, who had a little business going on the side with a kiddie-porn merchant—he was the other guy the cops were leading away in handcuffs tonight. He sold Miller the pictures and told him where to find Jonathan, information Barry's girlfriend had gotten out of Barry and handed to her partner." He glanced up. "Speak of the devil!"

"Who? The porn merchant?" David said and turned.

"How are the patients?" Sergeant Mooney said as he strolled up.

"Well, here's one of them," Patrick said as Jonathan came down the hall with one of the doctors. He got up and walked towards them. "How are you, son?" His voice almost cracked.

"I'm okay. He—the man who took me to the apartment didn't do anything. I got away from him," he added proudly.

"You're a bright, resourceful boy," the doctor said.

Patrick looked at him. "Is that right? Everything's okay?"

"Absolutely—physically, that is. We may recommend a counselor, but I'll talk to you about that later." He nodded at them and left.

Jonathan took his father's hand. "How's Mother?"

"I'm pretty sure she's going to be all right," Patrick said.

"You know your mother was pretty near to finding you when the fire started and the fire engines came," Mooney said. "And she wasn't feeling too hot, either. That took a lot of courage."

"Yeah," Jonathan said. Then he blurted out, "She drinks a lot." The bald statement lay there. "Maybe if she didn't drink so much I wouldn't have got stolen."

"Don't pin that on her," Mooney said. "She does her best. And she wasn't responsible for Lawrence Miller, the guy who abducted you, hanging around where you lived."

Patrick sighed. "I'm afraid that's my doing, not your mother's."

"No," Jonathan said.

"Yes." Patrick took a breath, and as simply as he could described the link between the pictures he had had Barry take and the man who had kidnapped him. "So you see, you can't blame that on your mother. Okay?"

Jonathan nodded. "Okay." After a pause he added, "I'm glad."

Martha came down the hall. She looked white with fatigue.

"What is it Jonathan can't blame on me?" she said. "It must be one of the few things he can't." There was bitterness in her voice.

Patrick turned to her. "I was telling Jonathan about Barry's taking the photographs and showing them to Cheryl and her selling them to Ben. By the way," he said, turning back to Mooney, "whatever happened to Cheryl?"

"She came to a bad end, I'm afraid. A former, er, business associate did away with her, and then went to her apartment to steal her photographs and negatives. It seems that Ben himself suggested he get the pictures back after Jonathan's kidnapping hit the news. But Leo was a clumsy burglar. It wasn't really his line of work. Neighbors heard him and called the police. The boys in blue turned up and brought him in. That's when the pieces started coming together."

David was looking at Martha. "What's going to happen now?"

She gave a tired smile. "I guess you and Patrick and Jonathan will get what you want. The doctors in here painted some unpretty pictures. They want me to get properly detoxed here and then go to a rehab."

David looked at her. "Will you?"

"Yes. I can't—I can't kid myself any longer." She took a

breath. "I'm going to need some things," she started, and then hesitated.

"We'll get them for you," Patrick said, looking down at Jonathan. "And we'll keep an eye on the apartment, won't we?"

"Sure." He was holding hard to his father's hand.

Martha looked at her former husband. "You'll be staying home—not traveling, I mean—while I'm in the rehab, won't you?"

"I will. I promise." He glanced down at his son. "We have some catching up to do."

"Afterwards," Martha started, then lost heart. After tonight, did she have any rights left?

"We'll worry about afterwards afterwards," Patrick said.

"Will you stay in your apartment or in ours?" Martha asked.

"I think it'd be a good idea for Jonathan to be in a different environment for a while," Patrick said.

"What about school?" Jonathan asked.

"There're such things as subways, even cars," Patrick said. "We'll work it out."

"You look dead on your feet," David said. "Go back and get some sleep. I'll come by and see you tomorrow."

"Thank you, David." Later, when she felt less awful, she'd be properly grateful. She knew he had eased the way for the hospital to get her into a rehab two thirds across the country—the same one he had been in. And he and they and the doctors had said three months. . . . But when they had talked to her about this a few minutes ago he had also said, "Don't think about it now. Take it a day at a time." Then he smiled. "You can take almost anything for a day."

"Anything" would include not seeing Jonathan for as long as she was away. After the past months, would he care?

"Jonathan," she said, and walked hesitantly over to him. She was desperately afraid he would back away.

But he didn't.

As Martha approached, Patrick moved from Jonathan's

side, leaving him free. Still Jonathan didn't move. Martha
came up and put her hands on his shoulders. "I'm sorry,
darling," she said. "I'll get better. You'll see. I promise."

Despite her pallor and the fatigue that made wrinkles under her eyes, she looked more like the mother he remembered with love and pain.

He put his hands on her arms. "Mom, get well soon."

"I will, darling. I will." She couldn't stop the tears, but
she wiped them away. Leaning forward, she hugged him and
felt his boy's lips kiss her cheek. "I'll write," she said.

She turned and looked at Patrick for a minute.

"We'll be fine," he said. "And don't worry about anything—if you can manage it."

"If I can manage it, I won't," she replied gravely.

She turned to David. "Thanks. I—I haven't always been
very grateful. But I am now. Or at least—I will be."

He smiled. "I'll be in touch."

Then Martha turned and walked away from them, down
the hall to begin her own long journey back.